THE SANDLOT SPIRIT

THE SANDLOT SPIRIT

A Story of Kids, Noise, and the Game That Wouldn't Sit Still

Book Three of The Sandlot Series

WALTER A. BEEDE

Beede Baseball Publishing LLC

Dedication

For every parent who ever drove home from a tournament doing silent math on the steering wheel and wondered, What are we doing?
For the mothers and fathers who still believe a game is something you play with friends on a field, not something you buy in monthly payments.
For the mentors who never charged by the hour, and the children who just
wanted to stay until it was too dark to see the ball.

The Sandlot Series

Prequel: Beneath the Home Run Sky

Book One: The Sandlot Promise

Book Two: The Sandlot Legacy

Book Three: The Sandlot Spirit

Series Note

The Sandlot Spirit is Book Three of The Sandlot Series. It is designed to stand on its own, but it carries the full weight of the books before it.

Beneath the Home Run Sky shows the earliest roots of Cedarbrook: the rough field, George's early field log, and the working-class families who first made room for children to play.

The Sandlot Promise follows the winter of 1969–70, when the field is reclaimed through grief and the fence becomes a line of protection. The Sandlot Legacy carries Cedarbrook through 1981, when Jack Thompson learns that keeping a field alive is also a way of keeping a promise alive.

This book moves the story into 1999, when youth baseball is changing around the Ruggiero family. Jack is no longer the boy at the fence. He is the steward of the field, and Cedarbrook must answer a new question: what happens when the game becomes something families are asked to buy instead of something children are allowed to love?

Reflective Prelude — The Sign-Up Night

,

1999

BEFORE THE FENCE, THERE had been the field. Long before parents stood in lines beneath academy banners, Cedarbrook had been a rough patch of dirt, chalk, and borrowed daylight — the kind of place Fred Davis and George Davis first marked out because a town needed somewhere for children to run toward instead of away.

Thirty years earlier, one bad night had changed the town. That night had sirens in it, and a parking lot, and names people still lowered their voices around. Afterward came the fence by the creek, built board by board after Fred's death because George Davis needed to reclaim the old field and draw a line children could trust. George had kept the early field log. Mary Davis kept the later ledger from her kitchen table, starting in December of 1969 and carrying it almost thirty years, until the winter before she died. By the spring of 1982, George was gone, and the town tried to rename what it had inherited. Jack Thompson dragged the infield on Wednesdays. Children kept finding the gate. The fence weathered, lost a board now and then, and got a new one nailed in by whichever set of hands was nearest. Hartwell took the corporation's offer and built somewhere else. The marsh gave back a few feet on bad winters and took them again in spring. The carved initials in the right-field corner stayed where they were.

This night did not look like that. No sirens. No blood. No reporter's voice. Just fluorescent lights buzzing in a middle school cafeteria and a line of parents trying to act like they were only there to sign a form.

The room smelled of floor wax, wet coats, and cheap pizza gone cold at the edges. On the far wall a vinyl banner sagged between two strips of duct tape:

NORTH SHORE ELITE BASEBALL ACADEMY

TRYOUTS · SHOWCASES · COLLEGE EXPOSURE

"Elite" and "Exposure" were twice as big as everything else. The banner drooped a little in the middle.

Tommy Ruggiero stood halfway down the line, a clipboard balanced on his forearm, a registration packet pressed to his chest. His winter coat hung open. But sweat prickled under his collar. The fingers of his right hand flexed inside a pair of cheap leather gloves, the kind you grabbed at the hardware store on the way to somewhere more important.

Tyler swung his legs from a plastic chair a few feet away, a scuffed wiffle ball pinched between his palms. Every few seconds he tossed it straight up, caught it, and squeezed.

Kyle stood in front of Tommy, hat brim bent just right, new sneakers squeaking on the waxed floor.

His number didn't exist yet, but his name was already printed in block letters at the top of the form.

Laughter ping-ponged off the tile—parents making light of schedules and carpools and "it'll all be worth it"—while forms were folded, unfolded, and smoothed flat again.

Ahead of them, two men in academy pullovers worked the folding tables with the easy patter of people who had said the same thing a hundred times.

"This is how it works now," one of them said, voice carrying just enough to sound official. "If your son wants the next level, we can put him on that track."

The word roadmap bumped hard against Tommy's rib cage. His father had called it a chance. His grandfather would have called it a blessing and gone back to his shift. He looked down at the registration form. Three neat columns marched across the page: TEAM PACKAGE WINTER TRAINING ADD-ON SHOWCASE OPTION Each column had little empty boxes beside bolded prices. Someone had chosen a font that made the numbers look thinner than they were, as if they might hurt less that way. At the bottom, PAYMENT PLANS AVAILABLE sat in friendly italics, like the station offering to float you a little more gas until payday.

Behind them, another family joined the line. The dad wore a work shirt with a company logo still stitched above his heart. The mom clutched a purse to her stomach, bracing for impact. Their son held a bat bag that dragged his shoulder slightly lower on one side.

"Three teams already filled," a mom a few spots back said, not quite quietly enough. "Coach said if we wait, we'll miss our window."

"College coaches were at their sixteen-U games last year," another added. "He said two kids committed before school even started."

Committed. Tommy had grown up hearing that word in church and hospital waiting rooms. Here it came with a price.

Tyler hopped off his chair and nudged his way back to Tommy's side. "Is this where the teams are?" he asked, eyes sweeping the room, taking in the banner, the tables, the line of fathers doing silent math in their heads.

"This is where they start," Tommy said.

Kyle licked his lips and tried to stand taller. "What if I don't make it?" he asked, voice pitched low, meant only for the three of them.

"You will," Tommy said too quickly. "You've earned your shot."

Karyn shifted her purse from one shoulder to the other. She'd been quiet since they walked in, eyes not on the banner or the brochures but on the boys. "Do they have to decide everything tonight?" she asked.

"The director said spots go fast," Tommy answered, nodding toward the front. "If we wait, we might not get in."

The line shuffled forward. Flyers for "Arm Care Protocol," "Mental Performance Training," and "College Exposure Weekends" sat fanned across the tables. A portable speaker near the far wall played walk-up music on low volume, the same eight bars of three different songs over and over.

Tyler's wiffle ball rolled away and bumped against the sneakers of a boy in front of them. The boy picked it up and flipped it back with an easy wrist. "You play?" he asked Tyler. "When they let me," Tyler said. The boy grinned. "They always let the little brothers catch bullpen." Tommy smiled despite himself. On the far wall, a District poster hung slightly crooked: SUPPORT YOUR COMMUNITY FIELDS. Two kids played catch beneath a chain-link backstop while somebody's uncle dragged a rake around the basepaths.

"Next," someone called. They were at the table now. The academy logo was crisp on the banner, crisp on the brochures, crisp on the man's pullover. The smile he wore had probably been practiced in a mirror until it landed right on the line between friendly and authoritative.

"Name?" he asked.

"Kyle Ruggiero," Kyle said, trying to make his voice sound determined instead of twelve.

"Position?"

"First base. Pitcher. I can play outfield too."

"Versatile. Good," the man said, already writing. "Birthdate?"

"November fourteenth, nineteen ninety."

"Perfect. That puts you as a rising nine," he said. "Those are key years if you want to build a real profile."

Karyn's eyes flicked up.

The man slid the clipboard toward Tommy and tapped the three columns with his pen.

"So," he said. "We've got our Team Package, which covers league play and in-season practices. Most serious families pair that with the Winter Training Add-On—that's reps, arm care, strength. And for our top-track guys, we recommend the Showcase Option. That's where the real exposure happens. College coaches. Radar guns. Video."

He said serious families like it was a compliment and a warning at the same time.

Tommy's hand hovered over the checkboxes. He thought of overtime settling into his lower back, of Kyle at three throwing rolled-up socks at the couch, and of Jack saying, "Well, that's a gift you don't ignore."

Tommy checked the first box. TEAM PACKAGE. "Good choice," the man said, too quick. "You don't want him chasing from behind all spring."

Tommy checked the second. WINTER TRAINING ADD-ON. He hesitated at the third. The number beside SHOWCASE OPTION sat there in ink that was not thinner than the others, no matter what the font tried to pretend. He saw it as miles of highway, hotel fees, fast-food dinners eaten in uniform pants, the quiet sting of a credit-card bill arriving three weeks after the tournament medals were hung on a bedroom doorknob.

Beside him, Kyle shifted, eyes flicking between the clipboard and the banner. Tyler pinched his wiffle ball until his knuckles whitened.

Karyn's hand rested flat on the table, fingers splayed like she might steady something if it started to tip.

The man leaned in as if he were doing Tommy a favor. "These are the years that move fast," he said. "If the boy can play and you're ready to back it, we'll put him in front of people."

He checked the third box. SHOWCASE OPTION. Karyn exhaled, small and almost inaudible.

"Excellent," the man said, flipping the form to the payment section. "You're doing the right thing. A few years from now you'll be glad you didn't wait."

Tommy nodded, but his eyes never quite found Karyn's.

When they stepped back into the parking lot, the winter air hit their faces like a reminder that it was still only February. Their breath smoked in the cold. Inside, the line kept moving, new families stepping up to the table, pens already poised.

"Can we go hit?" Kyle asked, already wearing the new academy hat like it had come with the form. "In the cage?" Tyler added. "Tomorrow," Tommy said. "We've got time."

Tyler bounced the wiffle ball off the hood and caught it. Across the lot, beyond the school and strip mall, Cedarbrook held against the sky.

Chapter One — The Tryout

Early Spring 1999 · North Shore Elite Fieldhouse

BY THE TIME THEY pulled off Route 1 and threaded through the back of the industrial park, the snow left in the shaded corners of the lots had gone the color of coffee grounds. Piles of plowed ice slumped against chain-link fences, streaked with sand and exhaust, winter refusing to admit defeat.

The North Shore Elite Fieldhouse didn't look like a place where a kid's dreams were supposed to start. It looked like every other warehouse on the row—gray metal siding, a loading dock, three dented bay doors, a tired sign that might once have advertised flooring or plumbing supplies.

Only the banner gave it away:

NORTH SHORE ELITE BASEBALL ACADEMY

TRYOUT TODAY — CHECK IN AT FRONT DESK

It fluttered in the March wind above a single glass door, corners snapping like a flag that hadn't decided which way to fly.

Tommy eased the car into a space between a contractor's pickup and a minivan that still wore last summer's camp sticker on the rear window. He killed the engine and sat for half a heartbeat longer than he needed to, fingers resting on the keys.

In the back seat, Kyle already had his cleats in his hands. He'd worn sneakers like they'd talked about—no sense dulling spikes on concrete—but the cleats were laced and ready, hanging by their tied-together tongues from his fingers like a promise.

"You're early," Karyn said, checking the dashboard clock. "Tryout doesn't start for twenty minutes."

"Coach said, 'Get there early or get left behind,' " Tommy answered. "Figured we'd vote on which one we wanted."

Tyler leaned forward between the seats, eyes on the warehouse. "Do they have real dirt in there?" he asked. "Or is it all carpet?"

"Turf," Kyle corrected automatically. "They called it a turf surface."

Tyler scrunched his nose. "So... carpet."

Despite the knot in his stomach, Tommy smiled. "Let's go find out," he said.

The wind slapped them the second the doors opened, snatching at caps and jacket hems. The parking lot was filling fast—sedans slipping into tight spots, SUVs nosing in wherever a painted line even hinted at permission. Dads carried bat bags over one shoulder like duffels. Mothers clutched coffees and clipboards. Kids walked somewhere between a march and a shuffle.

A strip of orange tape marked the entrance on the glass door. The glass was fogged halfway up from the heat inside.

The fieldhouse smell hit them in a rush: rubber pellets, old sweat, pine tar, leather, and something industrial underneath—machine oil or floor cleaner—that didn't belong anywhere near a sky. Voices bounced off metal rafters, a hundred conversations folding into a single tinny roar.

"Check-in table's over there," Karyn said, pointing with her chin. A long folding table ran along the far wall, staffed by two men and a woman in North Shore Elite pullovers. A handwritten sign read A–L on one half, M–Z on the other. Behind them, a portable whiteboard leaned against a column, the words 60-YARD · V-LO · POP TIME · EXIT VELO written in thick black marker.

"Go with Dad," Karyn told Kyle. "I'll grab a spot on the bleachers."

Behind the net, a rectangle of turf stretched forty yards under a ceiling that dipped just low enough to remind you this was still a building. Smaller cages lined the other side like horse stalls.

Tommy and Kyle joined the line at A–L. Tyler skipped sideways between them, the wiffle ball in his pocket thumping against his leg.

"Last name?" the woman at the table asked when they reached the front. "Ruggiero," Tommy said. "Kyle."

She slid a finger down a printed list, grabbed a Sharpie and a strip of athletic tape. In three practiced strokes she wrote 27 and slapped the tape onto the front of Kyle's shirt.

"There you go, twenty-seven," she said, already moving to the next name. "Pitcher, right?" "Pitcher and first base," Kyle said.

"Good," she answered, without looking up. "Go see Coach Martins for warm-ups."

She gestured toward the heart of the noise. The main turf lane had been turned into a measuring tunnel. At the far end, a screen with a hole cut in the middle waited; behind it, a radar gun sat on a tripod, pointed at whoever dared to throw. Halfway down the tunnel, another coach held a laminated clipboard and a stopwatch. Off to the side, cones marked starting lines for the sixty-yard dash.

Kyle's cleats clicked on the concrete as they headed toward the turf. "Hey," Tommy said, bending so only Kyle could hear him. "What do you own today?"

"My effort," Kyle said.

"Right," Tommy said. "Radar gun doesn't decide who you are." Kyle nodded, but his eyes had already slid toward the screen at the far end, toward the guy in the academy pullover calling out numbers that made other dads straighten or sag.

"Twenty-three, you're up!" someone shouted. A boy with 23 taped to his chest jogged onto the turf, shoulders tight, hat brim pulled low. He wound up and let the ball go, the sound of leather on mesh swallowed by the buzz of lights overhead.

"Sixty-three!" the coach behind the net called out. The boy's father let his shoulders drop half an inch.

Tommy swallowed. "Twenty-four, on deck! Twenty-five, get loose!" A coach with a whistle and a shaved head clapped his hands to gather the next cluster of boys.

"If you're twenty-six through thirty, over here!" he barked.

Kyle checked his tape. "That's me," he said.

Tommy touched the brim of Kyle's hat, a small correction to a bend that had tried too hard to be tough.

"Go be yourself," he said. "That's enough." Kyle jogged over to the group, joining a half circle of boys who looked, in the quiet between shouts, exactly like every boy who had ever waited to be picked: a little pale, a little wired, suddenly very aware of where their hands were supposed to go.

From the bench, Karyn watched them all, arms folded tight. Tyler sat beside her, swinging his feet, eyes tracking every throw.

"Which one is he?" asked the mother to her right, voice just loud enough to be polite.

"Twenty-seven," Karyn said. "The one with the navy undershirt."

"He looks good," the woman said. "My oldest is twenty-eight. They said this is his 'critical window.' " She rolled the phrase like something she'd practiced. "Hard to know what that even means."

A whistle blew. "All right, twenty-six through thirty, line up on the foul line!" Coach Whistle shouted. "Sixty-yard times first, then throws. When you finish, grab your gloves and head to Cage Three for exit velo."

The boys shuffled into a line at the edge of the turf. Another coach walked down, writing numbers next to names on a clipboard.

"On my whistle," he said. "You run straight through the cone at the end. Don't slow down until you hear me yell stop."

"Do we get more than one?" a boy asked. "You get what you get," the coach said. "Make it count." The first kid sprinted, sneakers slapping, arms pumping. The stopwatch beeped.

"Seven-six-three," the coach called, pen already scratching. "Next!"

"Seven-six-three," the kid repeated under his breath, like he'd just been handed his identity for the year.

When it was Kyle's turn, he stepped to the line and shook out his hands. Tommy could see his son's chest rising too fast under the number.

The whistle blew. Kyle exploded forward, knees driving, arms cutting. Halfway down the lane, his stride lengthened, that easy longdistance run he got from Karyn taking over, the kind that made gym teachers grin and other kids pretend not to mind.

"Seven-one-nine," the coach said when the stopwatch beeped. He wrote it down without looking up. They moved on to the throwing lane.

"Twenty-seven, you're on the mound," came the call. The mound was a worn-down portable slope, its green surface chewed up by months of spikes. A bucket of baseballs sat at the base. Behind the net, the radar gun's red eye waited, indifferent. "Warm up with two," the shagging coach said. "Then we'll start reading."

Kyle picked up a ball, bounced it twice in his hand, then found the seams and started his motion. His windup was the same one he used at Veterans—no added flourish, no extra coil—just a simple turn, stride, and whip.

The ball cracked into the screen. "Sixty-eight," the gun said in red digits. The coach glanced back. "Not bad," he said. "You've got more."

Second pitch. Same motion, a fraction more intent.

"Seventy." A couple of dads murmured.

"Third and final," the shagging coach said. "Make it smooth. Don't overthrow."

Kyle rolled his shoulders once and let his breath out slowly. For one heartbeat, the warehouse ceiling, the radar, the benches full of parents all fell away. It was just a boy, a ball, and a target.

He threw. The sound was sharper this time, less thud and more crack. "Seventy-two!" the coach behind the net called, louder now. "Nice arm, twenty-seven."

A few heads turned.

On the bench, Tyler punched the air. "That was awesome," he said. "Did you hear him? Seventy-two."

Karyn smiled, but the lines at the corners of her mouth didn't smooth. "They see how small he still is under that number?" she asked quietly. "Or just the gun reading?" Tyler didn't answer. He was already tracking the next kid.

When the throwing was done, the group was herded toward Cage Three. A tee, a net, and a machine that looked like a cross between a microwave and a science project waited for them.

"Exit velocity station," a younger coach said. "Three swings each. We're looking for how the ball comes off your bat."

"Load, swing through, and jog out," the coach said. "Don't admire it. There's a line behind you."

One by one they stepped in, set their feet on the painted marks, and took their cuts. The machine chirped after every swing, spitting out a number the coach wrote down without comment.

When it was Kyle's turn, he took his place in the box. The tee seemed a fraction too high; he adjusted it without being told. It was a small thing, but Tommy saw the coach watching him do it. First swing: solid contact, ball driving straight into the net.

"Sixty-one," the machine chirped. The coach wrote it down, unreadable. Second swing: a touch more aggressive, shoulders rotating, back hip driving. "Sixty-four." Tyler let out a soft whistle.

"Last one," the coach said. "Give me your best, twenty-seven." Kyle set the bat on his shoulder, breathed, and coiled. For the length of one heartbeat he wasn't standing in a warehouse with a number on his chest; he was back on the creek field with Jack and Tyler, dusk tugging shadows across the infield, the fence waiting beyond short left.

He swung like that. "Sixty-seven," the machine chirped, a shade brighter.

The coach allowed himself a small nod. "Nice piece," he said. "You keep eating and lifting, that'll jump in a hurry."

He scribbled something next to Kyle's name—an extra mark, an underline, Tommy couldn't tell— and moved on.

By the end of the session, the boys were a mix of sweat and jitters, caps pushed back, hair plastered to their foreheads. The coaches gathered them at midfield in a loose semicircle.

"You all did great today," the head instructor said, voice booming under the rafters. "We're going to take your numbers, your evaluations, and your age groups and build teams that will compete at the highest levels this summer. You'll get an email in the next week with your placement: Elite, Select, or Developmental."

The three words hung in the damp air like a ranking nobody had asked for.

"Parents," the coach continued, "we've got program packet folders up front—payment structures, practice schedules, showcase opportunities. Any questions, find a staff member in a pullover."

The herd broke. Kids drifted toward their parents, some walking taller, some shrinking into their hoodies. Moms and dads moved toward the table of packet folders, the rustle of paper blending with the thud of rolled-up turf in the next cage.

Kyle found them near the benches, cleats clicking on concrete again.

"So?" Tyler blurted. "What did they say? Did you hear your numbers? You were so fast, and your arm—"

Kyle shrugged, eyes bright. "It was... okay," he said, reaching for nonchalant and getting close. "Coach said I had a live arm."

"Live arm," Tyler repeated, grinning. "Like a firecracker."

Karyn brushed a bit of turf pellet off Kyle's cheek with her thumb. "You hungry?" she asked.

"We can grab pizza on the way home."

"Sure," Kyle said, but he was already looking back toward the whiteboard where a few coaches still stood, heads together over clipboards.

Tommy watched the coaches confer over their clipboards.

"You did good," Tommy told Kyle, resting a hand on his shoulder. "Whatever email comes, it doesn't change that."

Kyle nodded, still looking back toward the whiteboard.

They stepped out into the cold. The warehouse door thudded shut behind them. The late-afternoon light had gone thin and gray, the kind that made you feel farther from spring than the calendar claimed.

On the drive home, the boys argued softly in the back seat about Elite, Select, or maybe some secret tier above both. Tommy kept his eyes on the road.

Somewhere between Exit 43 and the rotary, his fingers tightened on the wheel.

NORTH SHORE ELITE—PARKING LOT, DUSK

The tryout ended the way storms ended — without an announcement, just a thinning of noise. Boys carried bats like they were carrying themselves.

Parents gathered in little triangles, pretending they were not counting. Kyle came out with his cap pulled low, cheeks still flushed from the cage, the strip of athletic tape with 27 on it half-peeled off his shirt. He found Tommy and Karyn by the car and his shoulders rose half an inch, the way they did when he had been holding something in.

A volunteer rolled a corkboard to the entrance doors and clipped up a sheet of paper. It wasn't on letterhead. Just names in columns, black ink, the kind of neatness that makes people believe it's fair.

Parents surged toward it. Tommy stayed where he was for a beat, the keys cold in his hand, then walked over.

His finger traced the page once, then again, faster. The second pass was the one that hurt. Ruggiero, K. A single letter beside the name: C.

Behind him, a father he didn't know was reading the same board out loud to his wife, voices carrying easily across the lot. Look at that. Cs are the developmental ones. They go on the bus to Worcester. The B kids get the showcases. The wife said something about a friend's son who had been a C the year before and was now nowhere. The man laughed once, not unkindly, the way you laugh at someone else's bad weather.

Coach Carver came out with a clipboard tucked under his arm. "Remember," he called, loud enough to carry, "C isn't a no. C is a commitment. Most of these guys play their way up. Some don't. Depends on the work."

Kyle had come up behind Tommy without him noticing. His eyes were on the board. Tommy could see the moment his son found his own name. The shoulders did the small thing shoulders do when a twelve-year-old has decided not to cry in a parking lot.

"It's just paper," Tommy said. The words came out smaller than he meant.

"Everyone's gonna know," Kyle said.

Karyn was beside them now, already reading faces. She put a hand on the back of Kyle's neck — light, warm, not pulling him anywhere.

Carver's voice floated over again, easy as ever. "We'll send the offers tonight. Twenty-four hours to secure your spot."

Tommy set his jaw. "We're doing it," he said.

Karyn looked at him. She didn't argue. She also didn't agree. She just kept her hand where it was on Kyle's neck, and the three of them walked back to the car together.

Chapter Two — The Empty Wednesday

Late Spring 1999 · Cedarbrook Field

ON THE FIRST WARM Wednesday of the year, Cedarbrook Field looked almost ready.

The last of the snow had retreated to thin strips along the outfield fence, and the infield was finally firm underfoot.

Jack Thompson's pickup rattled up the cracked driveway and eased into its usual spot beside the equipment shed. He cut the engine and sat for a second, fingers resting on the steering wheel, listening to how the place sounded when it was only breathing on its own.

The creek beyond center murmured in the distance. A gull screamed once over Route 1 and was gone.

Somewhere behind the third-base line, a dog barked at nothing in particular. No kids yet.

Jack pushed the door open with his shoulder and climbed out. His knees made the small complaint they made now when the weather changed. He stretched his back, then walked around to the bed of the truck and pulled out the chalk liner and the rake. The motions were as familiar as tying his boots.

For thirty years, the only advertisement for a Wednesday game had been daylight and the sound of a ball hitting a glove.

This year, he hadn't trusted habit.

WEDNESDAY NIGHT BALL—ALL WELCOME

He'd thumbtacked the notices at the bakery, the hardware store, the pizza place, the laundromat, even the middle school bulletin board beside a glossy academy flyer.

At 4:12, the field belonged only to him. He walked the first-base line, boot toes nudging at the edge where grass met dirt.

He set the rake teeth along the edge and pulled, shaving back just enough to see the brown line clearly. Then he dragged the rake across the infield, long even strokes that left soft furrows in the dirt. When he finished, he rolled the chalk liner out, filled it from the bag in the shed. And walked the baselines slow and steady.

By the time he was done, the diamond glowed as white and crisp as a clean scorecard. He stepped back, wiped his hands on his jeans, and looked around.

Still no kids. The scoreboard sat dark beyond right-center.

A car turned off the main road and crawled past the field, then kept going. A minivan slowed at the stop sign by the park entrance. He recognized the driver; one of the dads who'd spent most of last summer in a lawn chair near third, calling out reminders about cutoffs between sips of Dunkin.

The man saw Jack and lifted two fingers in a quick half-wave. Jack raised the rake in return.

The minivan blinked its turn signal toward the highway instead of the parking lot and eased away.

"Got somewhere else to be," Jack said softly.

He pulled his keys out, set them on the bleacher rail. The St. Christopher his father had carried in the GE plant for thirty-six years still hung from the ring, brass worn pale where Anthony Thompson's thumb had rubbed it through one shift after another until there was no shift left to work. Six years gone now. Jack had stopped expecting the missing of him to soften. He just knew where to find the man on a Wednesday afternoon, and the answer was here.

He walked to the right-field corner where the fence turned back toward the creek. He brushed his fingers over the boards at eye level, feeling the familiar carved initials beneath his hand.

Fred Davis. George Davis. Michael Davis. Jack Thompson. "Still here," he said. "Just quieter."

The crunch of gravel on the driveway made him turn.

A bike rolled into view first, rusted frame, one handlebar grip missing, a baseball card still clipped to the back wheel by a faded clothespin.

The boy riding it wore his cap backward and his backpack slung low on one shoulder. When he saw Jack, he hopped off and let the bike coast to a stop against the bottom row of the bleachers.

"Hey, Coach," he called, a little out of breath. "You still doing the Wednesday thing?"

Jack felt his shoulders drop in something like relief. "Depends," he said. "You bring a glove, Reyes?"

Marco Reyes held up his hand, fingers shoved into the webbing of a beat-up mitt that had once been somebody's good leather before life and concrete yards got to it. "Always," Marco said.

"Then yeah," Jack answered. "We're doing the Wednesday thing." Marco jogged down to the dugout, vaulted over the low rail, and set his backpack on the bench like it belonged there.

"You the only one?" Jack asked, not unkindly. "Luis said he might come after he finishes his paper route," Marco said. "His mom took the car because his sister had dance."

"What about the others?" Jack asked.

Marco scratched at a divot in the dirt with the toe of his sneaker. "Dylan's got hitting at the academy," he said. "Evan's doing that speed camp thing. Gabe's on some strength program. Coach says if he does the travel team and the speed camp too, he could be 'something.' " Jack held a baseball for a second, feeling the seams press into his fingers. "He tell you're something now?" Jack asked.

Marco looked at the grass. "He tells me to hustle," he said.

Jack threw the ball back a little firmer. "You are something now," he said. "We can work on the rest."

Marco caught it clean and smiled despite himself. They started playing catch, easing the ball back and forth, the distance stretching slowly from shortstop to deep second to shallow right.

Marco's throw had a little tail to it, the kind Jack liked; it gave you something to read.

"You know the academy coach?" Marco asked between throws. "Know of him," Jack said. "He runs a tight ship."

"He's got a real radar gun," Marco said. "Sets it up in the cage. Everyone watches the numbers." "I bet they do," Jack said.

"He said if I came in this winter, he'd put me on a throwing plan and I'd add ten miles an hour," Marco went on. "Said that's the difference between getting looked at and getting ignored."

"What'd your mom say?" Jack asked. Marco caught the ball, turned it in his hand.

"She said we don't have radar gun money," he answered. "Said we got rent and gas and one pair of school shoes money."

He fired the ball back, a little harder than he meant to. Jack snagged it and let the sting sit in his palm.

"That's good money," Jack said. "Field doesn't care how fast you paid to throw."

He lobbed the ball back with a softer arc, giving Marco time to get under it.

A second kid eventually wandered in. Luis, true to Marco's prediction, tossed his rolled-up paper bag into a trash can on the way by and trotted toward the dugout.

"Sorry I'm late," he said. "Had to finish Maple Street. Mrs. Fiore kept me on the porch talking about her cat."

"What'd the cat do?" Jack asked. "Nothing," Luis said. "That's the problem."

By 5:05, it was just the three of them: two boys and a man on a field that could comfortably hold eighteen without even using the outfield.

"Guess it's two-on-one today," he said. "We can still make a game out of that."

Marco brightened. "Workups?" he asked. "Like last summer?" "Workups," Jack agreed. "You two against me. I'll hit, you field. If you get me, you switch. If I get on, I get to talk trash about how I could've signed for more money if somebody had had a radar gun back in '78."

Luis frowned. "What's a radar gun?" he asked. Marco laughed.

"It's the box that tells your dad if he should be happy or mad on the ride home from the academy," he said.

Jack winced, just slightly. "Out here," he said, "we let your arm tell the story, not a number." He walked to home with a bat over his shoulder, the familiar weight settling into his hands. Marco took short, eager steps at shortstop. Luis jogged out to right-center, the spot nobody ever picked first until someone hit a ball out there.

Jack dug a toe into the dirt, felt the plate with the edge of the bat, and tossed the ball into the air.

"Ready?" he called. "Always," Marco said. Luis cupped his glove to his mouth.

"Bring it," he yelled. The crack of the bat cut across the quiet like a church bell. A low line drive rocketed toward the hole between short and third. Marco broke on first movement, glove flashing, body leaving his feet in a kid-sized dive that felt like it lasted an hour. The ball smacked leather and stuck.

"Oh-ho," Jack said. "That play gets you a sausage sub and your picture on the wall." Marco popped up, grinning, and fired to first anyway, just to finish the thought. "Out!" Luis shouted.

They played like that, Jack trying to find the spaces two kids couldn't quite cover and the kids closing them one by one.

When Marco lost a fly ball in the sun and it dropped a step behind him, Jack exaggerated his trot to first and announced, "Should've signed me when they had the chance." When Luis charged a slow roller and barehanded it to Marco, Jack clapped so loud it startled a crow off the left-field foul pole.

After a while, they drifted back to the dugout bench, sweat ringing their hat brims, shirts clinging to their shoulders.

"Coach," Marco said, catching his breath. "My mom asked how much I had to pay you for this."

Jack leaned back against the dugout rail. "You don't," he said.

"She said nothing's free," Marco went on. "She said if the academy costs what it costs and this doesn't cost anything, there's probably a catch."

Jack chewed on the inside of his cheek. "Tell your mom she's right about one thing," he said. "There is a price." Marco's eyes flicked up.

"For what?" he asked. "For me," Jack said. "Every time you show up, you pay me." Marco and Luis exchanged a look.

"With what?" Luis asked, skeptical. Jack picked up the ball, rolled it across his knuckles, then held it up. "Noise," he said. "Grass stains. The look on your face when you make a good throw." Luis snorted.

"That's not money," he said. Jack smiled.

The boys didn't catch all of it, but they caught enough to file away for later.

"Now," Jack said, straightening. "Enough soapbox. Back to work. Reyes, you're gonna learn how to turn two with a ghost at second. Luis, you're about to find out what 'backup' really means."

They moved again. The field, which had felt too big for three people a moment ago, shrank around the drills. The spaces between baselines tightened. The outfield didn't seem quite so empty.

A car passed on the road. Farther away, faint and muffled, there was the echo of a bat hitting ball inside some metal building with no sky above it. For a second, the sounds overlapped.

By the time the sun slipped behind the line of trees beyond left, the boys were panting lightly, socks stained, palms dirty. Jack's shirt clung to his back in a way that told him he wasn't twenty anymore.

He walked to the mound and toed the rubber, just because. From there, the perspective hadn't changed in thirty years: plate, batter's box, fence, the town on the hill pretending it didn't see how much of its heart was nailed into those boards.

"Last one," he called. "Make it count." He hit a high pop between them. Marco and Luis both broke on first movement, then slowed, then called it together, laughing when the ball clanged off Marco's glove and thudded into Luis's. "Not pretty," Jack said. "But the out still goes in the book."

"What book?" Luis asked, tucking the ball beneath his arm. Jack patted his back pocket.

"The one in here," he said. "I keep it without a pen these days." They walked off together, three shadows stretching long over the infield. At the shed, Jack hung the rake and rolled the chalk liner back into its corner. The fresh lines he'd laid an hour earlier were already softening in the fading light. Edges always did.

Before leaving, he stopped once more at the fence and laid his palm against the board.

"They're in cages tonight," he said to the wood. "We'll be ready when one comes back."

He locked the shed and climbed into his truck.

KITCHEN TABLE—LATE NIGHT

The email came at 11:17 p.m., subject line screaming a promise:

WELCOME TO NORTH SHORE ELITE.

Karyn opened it with one hand and steadied the mug with the other. The kitchen smelled like dish soap and tiredness. Tommy was upstairs, breathing the heavy breath of a man who had worked overtime three nights running. The boys had been asleep since nine.

The attachment was a PDF: deposit due within twenty-four hours, mandatory training package, facility fee, uniform fee. Karyn scrolled, hoping for a line that said, Just kidding. Instead, she found the paragraph in small print: Spots may be reassigned at the discretion of the Academy if payment deadlines are not met.

She read it twice. The numbers did not get smaller on the second pass.

A second email landed three minutes later, from a name she halfrecognized — one of the Elite mothers, the kind of woman who organized herself in capital letters. SUBJECT: PARENT NETWORK — CONGRATULATIONS PLAYERS! The body listed everyone who had been placed, by tier, in alphabetical order. Cs are at the bottom but please — every one of these boys is a winner!! Karyn looked for Kyle's name. There it was, near the end: Ruggiero, Kyle — C.

She sat with the laptop's glow on her face and tried to think about the money. She did the math she did when bills came: the column on the left of the envelope, what was in the checking account; the column on the right, what was owed by Friday. The Academy fee did not fit on either side without making something else slide.

Tommy came down in his work T-shirt, hair flat on one side from the pillow.

"Couldn't sleep," he said.

"Look," she said.

He read it over her shoulder. He did not say anything for a while. He pulled out the other chair and sat.

"It's a mortgage," she said.

"It's twenty-four hours," he said.

"It's not just money," she said. "It's what we teach him by paying it."

Tommy didn't answer right away. He was looking at the parent network email, at the way the C names sat at the bottom of the list like a footnote.

Her finger hovered over SUBMIT. "We do it," she said finally, voice flat, "but we don't pretend it's normal."

Tommy nodded, the way you nod when you accept the cost before you've figured out how to pay it.

Karyn pressed SUBMIT. The portal chirped Thank you!, bright and innocent.

Chapter Three — The Mentor and the Manager

BY THE TIME THE minivans started coming back up Chestnut Street, the light over Cedarbrook Field had gone soft and gold.

Jack Thompson was alone at the fence, a hammer in his hand, his jacket zipped to his throat. He'd spent the last hour resetting a board that had loosened where kids climbed over instead of using the gate. Habit more than necessity. He fenced when he needed to think.

Beyond the marsh, the academy lights were already on.

Jack sank the last nail and stepped back. The board sat flush with its neighbors, grain lined up, initials from three decades ago still visible on the slats above.

Fred Davis. George Davis. Michael Davis. Jack Thompson. He thumbed the carvings once, the way other men worked rosary beads, then wiped his palm on his jeans when he heard tires crunch on the gravel drive.

A familiar minivan eased into the lot and rolled to a stop beside his truck. The engine cut. For a second, nobody moved. Then the driver's door opened and Tommy Ruggiero climbed out, academy hat low over his brow. He held a folder in one hand, a coffee in the other, like he wasn't sure which one he trusted less.

"Thought you might be down here," Tommy said.

Jack set the hammer on the fence rail. "Where else would I be on a night like this?" he asked. "How'd the big meeting go?"

Tommy blew out a breath that came out closer to a laugh. "Depends who you ask," he said. "If you ask Coach Rick, we're all about to be drafted in the third round and retire our parents."

He held up the folder. The academy logo was glossy on the front, a stylized silhouette of a batter mid-swing over the words BASEBALL

FUTURES.

Jack nodded at it. "They give you that free," he said, "or is it on the payment plan?" Tommy smirked despite himself.

"Pretty sure they build it into the Gold Package," he said. "Along with the walking tour of the promised land."

He came to lean against the fence beside Jack. For a moment they just watched the field: the chalked lines from last night's town game still faintly visible, the mound scarred with cleat cuts, the grass along the baselines trying to grow into where it didn't belong.

"How'd Kyle throw?" Jack asked. Tommy's jaw worked once before he answered. "Good," he said. "Real good. Hit seventy-two on their gun." Jack let that number sit.

"That's a live arm," he said finally. "I ever tell you I signed with the Cubs for a sandwich and a bus ticket?"

"Couple hundred times," Tommy said, though the corner of his mouth twitched. "They made a big deal out of the gun tonight. Velo this, velo that. 'We'll get him on a plan. Add ten miles an hour. College coaches notice those numbers.' " He mimicked the cadence of the academy director without meaning to. Jack picked up the hammer again, turning it in his hands by the worn wooden handle.

"Sounds like quite a show," he said. "You go too?" Tommy nodded.

"Yeah," he said. "Karyn had a double shift at the hospital. Figured one of us ought to see what we're paying for."

He tipped his head toward the lights beyond the marsh. "You want the quick version?" he asked.

"I want the truth," Jack said. "Speed it comes in is your call." Tommy stared out at center field, at the dark line of trees beyond the fence.

"Bronze, Silver, Gold," he said. "Practices and local tournaments, then exposure events and video, then the full treatment—priority placement, recruiting help, the whole bit. Bronze is already a stretch. Silver means pushing the card harder than we should. Gold..." He shook his head. "Gold is for people in the front row."

"Fun was a bullet point," he said. "Under 'culture.' Somewhere between 'professionalism' and 'compete level.' " A breeze flicked the top leaves of the big maple behind third, carrying the faint sound of traffic from the highway.

"You believe him?" Jack asked, softly. Tommy was quiet for a long beat.

"I believe Kyle's good," he said. "I believe there are people in that building who know what they're doing. And I believe they're real good at making a guy like me feel like if I don't push every chip in right now, I'm failing my kid."

He let that settle, then added, "That's the part I don't like."

Jack nodded slowly, then asked, "How'd Kyle take it?"

"Tall when they said seventy-two," Tommy answered. "Small when they talked about Elite versus Select versus Developmental. By the end, I think he was more worried about which group he'd land in than anything else."

He glanced at Jack. "What do you think?" he asked. "You've seen more of this than I have. Are we supposed to sign up for all of it? Some of it? None of it? I don't want to be stubborn just to be stubborn."

Jack set the hammer down and hooked his fingers over the fence. "You want the speech or the short version?" he asked.

"Short," Tommy said. "I just sat through ninety minutes of slides."

Jack nodded toward the field. "Use what helps over there," he said. "Just don't hand them the keys to your whole house."

"Free," Tommy repeated. "I don't know if they even know that word over there."

Jack smiled. "Bring him down some night," he said. "Bring Tyler too. We'll take a look."

Tommy straightened.

"You'd do that?" he asked. "Even if he's on one of their teams?"

"Especially if he is," Jack said.

Tommy nodded, the decision settling somewhere behind his eyes. "I'll talk to Karyn," he said. "She still trusts you more than any brochure." "That just means she's met a lot of brochures," Jack said.

A car turned into the lot. The passenger door flew open before the wheels fully stopped. Tyler hopped out, wiffle ball in his hand, academy hat jammed down over his hair, Kyle climbing out behind him with a bat bag slung over one shoulder.

"Coach Jack!" Tyler called. "We came!" "I can see that," Jack said. "Good thing I didn't give your spots away." Kyle came up slower, eyes flicking from the fence to the field to his father. "Hey, Coach," he said.

"Hey yourself," Jack answered. "You bring that seventy-two with you, or did you leave it in the cage?"

Kyle blushed, but he smiled. "I brought my arm," he said. "The gun didn't fit in the car." Jack laughed.

"Good answer," he said. "Let's get some work in." Two nights later, Jack found himself in a different kind of room.

The middle school cafeteria looked smaller when it was full of folding chairs. Fluorescent lights buzzed overhead. At the front, a projector screen glowed with the academy logo, bright against the painted cinderblock wall.

Jack took a seat in the last row, ball cap low, jacket zipped. He hadn't planned on coming. Then he'd thought about all the parents who didn't have a Jack in their life. And he'd decided maybe he ought to see what they were being sold.

"Thank you all for coming out tonight," said the man at the front. Coach Rick Mancini. Quarter-zip pullover with the logo on the chest. Early forties, shoulders still broad, haircut that said he didn't pay for his own trims. His voice had just enough gravel to sound like it had once echoed in a dugout.

"I know your time is valuable," he went on, "and so is your investment in your sons' futures."

Jack felt, rather than saw, Tommy shift beside him at the word investment.

The slides went the way slides went. Bronze, Silver, Gold. Each tier a longer column of bullets. Each bullet a price. Rick's voice was easy and practiced and never once mentioned gas, missed dinners, or the look on a fourteen-year-old's face when he landed on the wrong side of a roster cut.

Jack watched the room as much as he watched the screen. He saw heads nodding at the words scholarships and exposure. He saw pens start to move the first time Rick said limited spots. He saw one mother glance at the prices, then at the floor, already calculating which bill could be paid a week late.

When the slide deck ended, there was a smattering of applause. Rick smiled, the kind of smile that lived halfway between coach and salesman.

"Staff at the back of the room with program packets," he said. "If you're ready to move forward tonight, we can get you signed up and make sure your son doesn't miss his window."

On the drive home, Tommy said very little. Jack said even less.

A week later, the light over Cedarbrook Field was good again. Jack dragged the infield and chalked the lines, the same way he always had. When he finished, he checked his watch.

4:58 p.m. He heard them before he saw them, the mix of voices and laughter and the sound of metal bats clanking against one another.

Tyler hit the grass at a dead run, wiffle ball already in his hand, then skidded to a stop just shy of the baselines. Kyle followed at a more measured pace, bat bag over his shoulder, academy hat in his hand instead of on his head. Behind them came Moose Donnelly, taller than both Ruggiero boys by a head, big hands already wrapped around his glove. Two more kids trailed in their wake, Marco and Luis, drawn back by habit and the promise of something that didn't come with a logo.

"You weren't kidding," Tommy said quietly as he took a spot along the fence with Karyn. "You really run this like a practice."

Jack stood near the mound with a bucket of balls at his feet. "Even better," he said. "I run it like a game that likes to pretend it's a practice."

He clapped his hands. "Alright, you maniacs," he called. "Infielders on the dirt, outfielders on the grass. We're gonna see if you remember how to move without a whistle."

They broke into positions like they'd been doing it for years. Kyle at second, Marco at short, Moose over at first, Luis in right, Tyler bouncing in left with too much energy and not enough body to hold it.

Jack picked up a ball. "No radar gun," he said. "No stopwatches. Just you, the ball, and the next right thing."

He rolled a slow grounder toward Marco. Marco charged, fielded clean, and fired to first. Moose caught it with soft hands.

"One," Jack said. "Again."

He hit another, this time to Kyle's backhand side. Kyle slid, planted, and turned to throw.

"Two," Jack said. "Make ten in a row look boring. Anyone can make one great play. College coaches fall in love with boring."

Tyler raised his hand from left. "Coach," he called. "They talk a lot over there—you know, the academy —about video and profiles and stuff. Does that really matter?" Jack sent a fly toward left-center. Luis sprinted over, called it, and squeezed it tight.

"Depends who you ask," Jack said. "You ask the guy selling the package, he'll tell you profiles are everything. You ask the guy trying to win a ballgame, he'll tell you he likes the kid who hits the cutoff and backs up first on a Tuesday in April."

Tyler jogged the ball back in. "So what are they really looking for?" he asked. "Depends which they you mean," Jack said. "The ones in quarter-zips or the ones in dugouts."

Kyle smirked, but he was listening, too. "Dugout theys," Tyler said.

Jack lobbed another grounder, this time between Kyle and Marco. They collided, laughed, and still managed to shovel the ball to Moose.

"Dugout theys are looking for kids they can trust," Jack said. "The ones who show up, learn fast, and don't disappear on a bad day."

"It's better than okay," he said. "You run hard, you listen, you help the younger kids, and you keep loving the game, any college worth your time will be lucky to have you. Whether you trained at an academy, a sandlot, or a parking lot is about tenth on their list."

Tyler nodded, shoulders loosening.

"How about you, Kyle?" Jack asked. "How's it feel here?" Kyle hesitated, eyes on his glove.

"I like it better," he admitted. "It doesn't hurt as much." Jack filed that away.

"Good note," he said. He looked around for a moment without saying more, then tossed the ball back into the bucket.

As the sun slid down behind the treeline, the field caught the last of the light, dirt and grass holding it in the way they always did, the fence casting long, steady shadows.

Out beyond the marsh, the academy lights clicked on.

Down at Veterans, a ball skipped off the edge of the grass and took a bad hop. Moose knocked it down with his chest, laughed, and fired to first anyway. Tyler picked it clean. Kyle, at second, yelled "Nice!" without thinking.

Jack watched Kyle charge a short hop and Tyler clap for him from left, and for a minute that was enough.

He picked up another ball and grinned. "Last set," he called. "Make it look boring."

The kids went back to work under a sky just starting to swallow the day. The old fence stood behind them. Beyond the marsh, the new lights hummed.

Chapter Four — The First Tournament

,

Early Spring 1999 · New England Baseball Challenge Complex

BY THE TIME THE alarm went off, it felt less like morning and more like they'd stepped into some other, dimly lit world where clocks didn't work right.

4:27 a.m. Tommy Ruggiero slapped at the nightstand until he found the button. The beeping stopped. The silence didn't feel any kinder. His eyes burned. His back ached from yesterday's shift. For a second he lay there, listening to the house.

The fridge hummed. The furnace clicked. Somewhere down the hall, Tyler's cough hiccupped once and settled.

Beside him, Karyn exhaled through her nose. "That's not a real time," she said into the pillow.

"Tournament says first game's at eight," Tommy replied. "Coach Rick wants them there an hour and a half early. 'Upper-deck warm-up,' he called it."

"You're the one who signed the form," she said, but there was no real bite. She pushed herself up on an elbow, hair falling into her face. "You make the coffee. I'll get the boys."

The kitchen smelled like cheap grounds and peanut butter a few minutes later. Karyn lined zip-top bags on the counter with the efficiency of someone who'd done it too often: sandwiches, fruit, granola bars,

Advil. A folded piece of paper sat by her elbow, numbers in her neat handwriting.

Gas. Hotel. Tournament fee. Jerseys. "Optional" T-shirt Tyler had begged for. She added a line for parking and put a question mark next to it.

"You don't have to keep that out," Tommy murmured, pouring coffee into mismatched travel mugs. "Yes, I do," Karyn said. "Otherwise it turns into air. Air's easy to spend."

Tyler shuffled in, cleats dangling from one hand, hoodie half-zipped over his NORTH SHORE ELITE shirt.

"Morning," he said, voice still thick with sleep.

"Brush your teeth," Karyn said automatically. "Then again before we leave. I don't want you breathing that hotel pillow back into the car for three hours tomorrow."

Kyle appeared behind him, rubbing one eye. His hoodie was blank; his Elite shirt was stuffed into his backpack instead. He'd insisted on that without quite explaining why.

"You don't have to come to all of it," Tommy said quietly to him. "You know that, right? You could stay with Nana."

Kyle shook his head. "I want to be there," he said. "Tyler'll need a catcher for warm-ups." Pride and worry landed at the same time in Tommy's chest.

They loaded the car in the dark—cooler, duffels, bat bag, Tyler's glove laid on top like something fragile—and pulled away from the curb at 5:05. Chestnut Street was empty. Cedarbrook Field lay under a skim of frost, the fence a darker line against pale grass.

"Looks cold," Tyler said, peering out the window.

"Field doesn't mind the cold," Tommy answered. "It minds being lonely." Karyn reached across and squeezed his knee.

They turned onto Route 1, then the highway that would take them north and west to the tournament complex, three towns and one state line away.

Welcome to the Circuit

The sun had climbed high enough to burn through the haze by the time they pulled into the sprawling lot of the New England Baseball Challenge Complex.

If Veterans Field was a homemade meal, this place was an all-you--can-eat buffet with a corporate logo: eight fields, each with its own digital scoreboard; batting cages lined up like carwash bays; a two-story building in the center housing a "Performance Center," "Recruiting Hub," and a pro shop big enough to clothe a small country.

Tyler pressed his forehead to the window. "Whoa."

Kyle tried to hide his own reaction with a shrug. "Looks like a mall," he said.

A staff member in a fluorescent vest waved them toward TEAM PARKING ONLY, then gestured at a sign: PARKING – $10 PER DAY—CASH ONLY. Karyn fished in her purse and handed Tommy a ten without looking at him.

"Add another line," she said.

They found the rest of the North Shore Elite team under a portable tent near Field 3. Coach Rick stood at the center, sunglasses on despite the overcast, clipboard in hand. Kids milled around him in matching navy hoodies, numbers on their backs, names on their sleeves.

"Ruggiero!" Rick called when he saw them. "Glad you made it. Ty, field's open. Go get loose. Kyle, right? You can help with bullpens."

Kyle nodded, chest tightening with a mix of yes and somehow. Parents clustered with coffee cups, folding chairs, and coolers. Tommy and Karyn set theirs a little apart from the main pack along the third-base line. They recognized some faces from town, others from tryouts and payment meetings. Snatches of conversation drifted back.

"Yeah, we went Gold. Can't mess around the 13U year, you know?"

"Rick says there'll be D-II and D-III guys walking around this weekend."

"Did you see the email about the recruiting seminar between games? We probably should go."

Tommy unfolded his chair and sat without quite joining in. Karyn stayed standing, arms folded, watching Tyler and Kyle in the warm-up pen.

Even from a distance, Tyler's motion had the fluidity that made him easy to spot. Kyle crouched behind the plate, glove popping with each pitch. From here, you couldn't see the slight wince when he turned his hand just so after the harder ones.

"You cold?" Tommy asked. "A little," Karyn said. He knew she meant more than the air.

Game One

Tyler got the ball for the first game, like Rick had promised. "Set the tone," Rick told him, thumb tapping the brim of Tyler's cap twice. "We win this pool, we're in the driver's seat. Attack the zone. Showcase the stuff."

Tyler nodded, wires buzzing through his limbs. Stuff. He rolled the word around in his mind. He'd never thought of what he threw as stuff. Just pitches. The ball. Him.

He took the mound against a team in bright red jerseys with an out--of-state name on the chest. Their parents carried clipboards with laminated rosters. Their head coach had a radar gun out before the first pitch.

"North Shore Elite," the PA announcer intoned through a crackling speaker. "Please welcome..." The first inning went by fast. Tyler struck out two and got a grounder to short. As he walked off, Rick leaned in again.

"Good," he said. "We're sitting seventy-four, seventy-five. Keep climbing." "Climbing what?" Tyler asked.

"Velocity," Rick said. "Stay tall. Drive. Don't pace yourself, we've got you for at least five."

Five. Tyler ran the math in his head: seven-inning game, pitch count limits treated like suggestions, two more games today if they kept winning. His chest tightened. He told himself not to be soft.

Between innings, Kyle grabbed his brother's warm-up tosses. Each throw thudded into his glove, reverberating up his arm. The turf mound felt harder than the one at Veterans, less forgiving. Music blasted from the central speakers, drowning out their usual small talk.

"You're doing great," Kyle said anyway. "Can't feel my legs," Tyler joked, but there was truth under it. By the fourth inning, Elite led 3–1.

Tyler had six strikeouts and one walk. His pitch count, according to the volunteer scorekeeper, had drifted higher than Tommy liked.

"He's getting up there," Tommy murmured. "Relax," said a dad in a Gold hoodie beside him. "This is what you pay for. Pressure. Competition. Rick knows what he's doing."

On the mound, Tyler missed high three times in a row. His front shoulder flew open sooner than it should, the way it did when he got tired. Kyle set up lower, trying to coax him back on line.

Rick called time and trotted out. Tommy held his breath. They talked for a moment, Tyler nodding along. Rick clapped him on the shoulder and jogged back, leaving Tyler in.

"Okay," Tommy said under his breath. "Okay." Tyler battled through two more innings, bending but not breaking. When he finally handed the ball over in the sixth with Elite still ahead 3–2, his arm felt distant, like it belonged to someone else.

They won, barely. A pop-out to first with the bases loaded ended it. "Great job, Ty!" parents called. "That's how you compete!"

Tommy and Karyn watched their son walk off with shoulders rounded a little more than usual.

"How you feeling?" Tommy asked when Tyler reached them. "Fine," Tyler said too quickly. "Rick says I might close the second game if we need it."

Karyn's eyes flicked to Tommy's. They shared the kind of look you only learn after a lot of years in the same small kitchen.

"Drink water," she told Tyler. "Stretch. And eat. Not just the sugar stuff." "Yes, ma'am," he said, forcing a grin.

Kyle sat down beside him on the grass, stretching his own legs. Catching had left his thighs buzzing and his thumb tender. He massaged it gently when no one was looking.

Between Games

There were two hours between Game One and Game Two. Not enough time to go anywhere. Plenty of time to spend more money.

Inside the main building, a college-aged kid in a polo at an information desk explained the seminar schedule.

"Our Director of College Placement is giving a talk at one o'clock," he said. "We'll go over how to market your son's metrics, all that. Free for Silver and Gold families, ten dollars for Bronze."

Karyn looked at Tyler, who sat at a nearby table with his head on his folded arms.

"I care about his elbow," she said quietly. Tommy nodded. They took their cooler to a patch of grass near the outer fence and made a picnic out of it. A few other families drifted over, drawn by the shade and the distance from constant announcements.

Marco's mother spread a blanket. Moose's dad produced a bag of orange slices.

"It's like Little League again," somebody said. "If Little League cost four hundred dollars to enter."

They laughed, but the joke sat heavy. Tyler picked at a sandwich. Kyle inhaled his, then stole half of Tyler's when his brother wasn't looking. "You nervous for Game Two?" Kyle asked.

"I'm fine," Tyler said. "It's just... it's a lot."

"A lot of what?" Tyler searched for the word. People. Noise. Expectation.

"Everything," he said at last.

Game Two

The second game started under a higher, harsher sun. Heat bounced off the artificial surface like somebody had turned the field into a low oven.

Tyler played short, which meant less throwing but more running. Kyle caught three innings, then moved to first. Their opponents this time were a local powerhouse in crisp white uniforms, parents in folding chairs with built-in shade canopies.

The game was tight from the start. Elite went down 2–0 in the first, tied it in the third, fell behind again in the fourth. By the fifth, Rick's jaw was working overtime.

In the top of the sixth, with two on and nobody out, he made his move. "Ty," he called, holding up a ball. "You ready to shut this down?" Tommy felt his stomach drop.

Tyler looked at the scoreboard, then at his coach, then toward his parents' chairs. From this distance he couldn't see their faces clearly, but he knew what he'd find there: pride, worry, a love that didn't always know where to sit.

"Yeah," he said. "I'm ready." He wasn't. His warm-ups sailed arm-side. The first batter walked on five pitches. The next poked a single through the right side. Suddenly it was 4–2 with the bases loaded and nobody out.

Rick paced at the top step, indecisive for the first time all day. "Come on, Ty," someone shouted. "You got this!"

Tyler tried to calm his breathing. He told himself to pretend it was Veterans—just Jack at the fence, just Kyle behind the plate. But the speakers were blaring between-pitch music, the other dugout was chanting, and a radar gun pointed at his back.

He left a fastball up. The hitter didn't miss. A line drive screamed into the gap. Two runs scored easily, a third on a relay that sailed up the line. 7–2. Rick finally came and took the ball.

Tyler handed it over and walked off to a smattering of polite applause. His arm felt like the inside had turned to sand.

On the bench, he sat with elbows on knees, head hanging.

Kyle eased down beside him. He wanted to say something clever, something to make it lighter, but nothing came.

"You're okay," he settled on. "It happens." Tyler didn't answer. They lost 9–3. The handshake line felt longer than the game.

Afterward, in the strip of shadow beneath the bleachers, Rick brought the team in close.

"Games like that are why we're here," he told them. "Pressure reveals character. We'll be better tomorrow. Second game in the pool. Win and we still advance. Lose and we go home early. So hydrate, eat right, get some sleep. Be ready."

Tyler nodded along, but the words slid over him like water over rock.

Hotel Night

They stayed because they'd already paid. The hotel was one of those off-the-highway places with carpets that had seen their share of cleats and coolers. The lobby smelled faintly of chlorine from the small indoor pool.

Tyler and Kyle dumped their bags in the room and made a beeline for the water.

"Thirty minutes," Karyn called. "Then showers and bed. We're leaving by seven."

The pool became a truce zone. Kids from three teams splashed and shouted, tournament results briefly irrelevant. Nobody cared who'd pitched well or swung through a fastball. They were just boys throwing a foam ball back and forth, timing jumps off the edge like dives into some other, easier childhood.

Tommy sat in a plastic chair, shoes off, socks damp from the splashes that found him. Another Elite dad sank into the chair beside him with a groan.

"Feels like I drove all day just to sit in a different folding chair," the man said.

Tommy laughed. "At least this one comes with free foot baths," he said, nodding at the water puddling under them.

"Worth every penny," the man replied, but his eyes drifted to his phone, where an email from the academy pinged in.

Tomorrow's bracket schedule. Notes about "playing for seeding." A reminder about next month's "optional but highly recommended" skills camp.

Upstairs later, Kyle lay in the second bed, ankle crossed over knee, trying to find a position where his knees didn't throb.

"Does it hurt?" Tyler asked from the other bed, staring at the popcorn ceiling. "Nah," Kyle lied.

"You sure?" "Yeah." Silence stretched.

"I'm sorry about the sixth," Tyler said quietly. "It's okay," Kyle answered. "Rick said the defense should have helped you more." "That's not what I mean."

Kyle rolled onto his side, looking at his brother's profile in the dim light from the parking lot. "What do you mean, then?"

"I let everything get loud," Tyler said. "The field, the other dugout, the gun. I started pitching to all of that instead of the mitt."

Kyle thought of Jack at Veterans, standing by the fence with his hands in his pockets, saying, Make it look boring.

"We get back to him tomorrow," Kyle said. "He'll cut it down for you." Tyler let out a breath. "One more game first," he said. "Then we go home."

Game Three

They lost the third game quietly the next morning, 5–1, to a team whose coach kept telling parents they were "small but scrappy" like it was a brand.

Tyler played third. Kyle caught four innings. Neither did anything remarkable enough to stick in the memory. They were both simply tired in that whole-body way kids weren't supposed to be yet.

When the last out dropped into the left fielder's glove, Rick gathered them down the line.

"Not the weekend we wanted," he said. "But this is why we train. This is why we push. We'll be back here next month for the Spring Kickoff Classic. We'll be ready."

Tommy listened, exhausted to the bone. Karyn stood beside him, the folded paper of expenses now creased and soft from being handled.

"Spring Kickoff Classic," she repeated under her breath. "We haven't even finished winter."

On the drive home, Tyler fell asleep before they hit the highway. Kyle watched stocky trees flick past, elbow propped against the window, forearm resting on a half-deflated travel pillow.

"You okay back there?" Tommy asked. "Yeah," Kyle said. He wasn't sure if it was true or if it just seemed easier than explaining. Karyn sat with the notebook open on her lap, pen hovering. After a long moment, she wrote a new line beneath the others.

First tournament: three games, two nights, four hundred and thirty-seven dollars. Then, after a beat, she added another in smaller letters.

Tyler's arm: sore. Kyle's knees: sore. Joy:? She closed the notebook and slid it back into her bag.

Back at the Fence

Cedarbrook Field looked almost surprised to see them that evening. The air had warmed. Snow lingered only in the shadows along the foul lines. The boards of the fence held the weak March light like they'd been hungry for it.

Jack was there, of course. He leaned against the first-base dugout, hands in his windbreaker pockets, like he'd never left.

"Hey," he called as the Ruggieros walked up from the lot. "How'd the big show go?" Tyler smirked. "We're not champions of anything."

"Not yet," Jack said. "Field's still here. That's a start." Kyle peeled off toward the dugout, tossing his bag down and kneeling to retie his cleats. Tyler hung back by the chalked first-base line.

"I pitched," he said. "Held them down in the first game. Got rocked in the second." Jack nodded. "Feels lousy, doesn't it?"

"Yeah." "Good," Jack said calmly. "It means you care. Now let's make sure we don't care about the wrong things."

Tyler frowned. "What do you mean?" Jack hooked a thumb toward the fence.

"You let the lights and the music and the gun get big in your head," he said. "They talk loud, those things. They tell you're only as good as your last number."

He pointed to the small rectangle of worn dirt in front of home plate. "But the game's still this," he said. "You and the ball and somebody trying to hit it or stop it. You keep that small and honest, you'll be fine."

Tyler looked at the plate, then back at Jack. "What if I don't get a scholarship if I don't go to every one of those tournaments?" he asked, the question finally breaking free. "What if I fall behind?"

"You won't," Jack said. "Not if you do the right work in the right places. That includes rest. That includes nights like this, where you're tired and you still show up because you love it, not because it's on a schedule."

He clapped Tyler lightly on the shoulder. "Come on," he said. "Let's play a little catch. Just you and me. No numbers."

They threw down the right-field line until the sun slipped behind the houses. Each toss loosened something in Tyler's chest. Each catch reminded him his arm still belonged to him, not to a radar gun or a bracket.

On the other side of the field, Karyn sat on the bleachers, shoulders dropped for the first time all weekend. Tommy stood at the fence with his hands on the rail, watching his boys move in the familiar rhythm of throw and catch.

The highway's distant hum provided a low backdrop. If there were lights on at the academy, they didn't show here.

When the ball slipped once and skittered toward the fence, Tyler chased it down and picked it up near the boards where three sets of initials were carved.

He ran a thumb under them, tracing the grooves.

"Maybe someday it'll be T. R. and K. R. up there," Jack called from the outfield.

Tyler smiled, tucking the ball into his glove. "Maybe," he said.

He turned, took his crow hop, and sent the ball back through the air with a clean, easy motion that had nothing to do with tournaments or Gold Packages and everything to do with a field that refused to forget what it had been built for.

Jack caught it with a sharp pop. "Better," he said. "Again."

They threw until it was too dark to see the seams, then stayed for one more toss anyway.

HOTEL HALLWAY—FIRST TOURNAMENT WEEKEND

The boys slept in a pile of limbs and duffel bags, a hotel-room sandlot built out of blankets. Down the hall, ice rattled in a machine that never stopped making it.

Tommy stepped out for air and found two fathers leaning near the stairwell, voices low, beer bottles sweating in their hands.

"Carver's kid got moved up," one said. "Didn't even play that well."

"Carver paid for the winter package," the other answered. "And he knows Collins. That's how it works."

Tommy stopped short, half-hidden by the soda machine. Names he'd heard in passing now sounded like gears.

"You gotta sponsor something," the first father went on. "Or you're just... you know. Another family."

"It's not bribery," the other said, laughing. "It's support."

A door clicked. The Ruggieros' room. Tommy turned and saw Tyler standing in the crack of it, eyes wide, pajama pants twisted at the ankle. Tyler had come for water and found a different kind of thirst.

The fathers noticed and went quiet, suddenly polite. "Hey, bud," one said, too cheerful. "Big day tomorrow."

Tyler nodded the way kids nod when they've decided not to say what they heard, then closed the door slowly. Tommy followed him back inside and shut the latch.

Karyn was a shape under the comforter, breathing the breath of someone who had learned to sleep through hallway sounds. Kyle was on the cot, mouth open. Tyler climbed back onto the queen bed and sat against the headboard with his knees up, the way he had when he was younger and there was a thunderstorm.

"What'd you hear?" Tommy asked, sitting down on the foot of the bed.

Tyler shrugged. The shrug was performance.

"Nothing," he said.

Tommy waited. In the dark, a boy's breathing tells you what he's trying not to say.

"They said you have to pay," Tyler whispered finally. "To move up."

Tommy thought for a long moment. He could give the clean answer. He could give the moral answer. Tyler was eleven; either would have worked. Instead he gave the honest one, because Tyler was eleven and would catch the lie.

"Sometimes," he said. "Sometimes people confuse paying with caring."

"So if we don't, I'm stuck."

"You're not stuck."

"Then why do they get to decide?"

Because grown-ups love order when it comes from a voice they will obey, Tommy almost said — then stopped himself, because that was the kind of sentence that made a kid feel preached at instead of helped.

He reached over and put his hand on Tyler's foot under the blanket. The foot was bony and warm. Tyler didn't pull it away.

"They decide on paper," Tommy said. "We decide in dirt."

Tyler didn't answer for a while. When he finally lay down and rolled toward the wall, Tommy stayed sitting on the foot of the bed for another minute, listening to the ice machine in the hallway. He didn't know yet whether what he had said was true. He just knew he wanted Tyler to grow up believing it could be.

Chapter Five — The Winter Cage

BY JANUARY, CEDARBROOK FIELD had gone quiet in the way only a New England field can.

The bases were stacked in the shed. The dugouts held nothing but a few forgotten paper cups and a rake leaning in the corner. Snow had come in uneven fits—enough to crust the infield, not enough to bury it. The fence stood in a shallow drift, boards silvered and stiff, initials softened under frost.

Jack Thompson walked the perimeter anyway. His boots left prints along the foul line. His breath made small clouds that vanished as soon as they formed. Now and then he nudged a loose board with the toe of his boot, more out of habit than need.

On some winter nights, if he stopped beside the third-base dugout and closed his eyes, he could almost hear it: ball on wood, kids shouting, the thud of feet rounding first. Ghost sounds. Honest ghosts.

Tonight, all he heard was the highway hum and the distant whine of the Academy's heating units across the marsh.

He turned his collar up against the wind and headed back to his truck. A glossy flyer lay on the passenger seat, North Shore Elite's logo stamped across the top.

WINTER PERFORMANCE PROGRAM Keep Your Player Ahead of the Curve Bullet points marched down the page: year-round development, professional instruction, maximize off-season gains. At the bottom, a line in bold: If you're not training, someone else is. Jack turned the flyer over, then back again, as if a different message might appear on the blank side.

It didn't. He folded it once and slid it into his jacket pocket without quite knowing why.

Indoor Season

The first winter night the Ruggieros walked into the Academy, the shock wasn't the size of the place. They'd seen that in the fall.

It was the air. Warm. Dry. Heavy with rubber and disinfectant. Fluorescent lights hummed overhead. Industrial fans pushed stale heat through long nets.

"Smells like a tire store," Kyle muttered. Tyler didn't answer. He was looking down the main hallway, where six batting tunnels stretched away. At the far end, a kid in a college hoodie took swings off a tee while a coach filmed from the side.

"Welcome, welcome!" Coach Rick's voice boomed as he strode toward them, hands spread wide. "Ruggiero boys, good to see you. Ready to get after it this winter?"

Tommy shifted the strap of the bat bag on his shoulder. "We're here," he said. "That's a start."

Karyn stood half a step behind the boys, folder clamped under her arm. Inside: the program contract and a copy of the payment plan. Bronze Winter Performance—two nights a week of hitting, throwing, and "mobility and strength components."

They'd sat at the kitchen table and circled the cheaper option in the lamplight, both saying the same word at the same time. "Bronze," Karyn had said. "Bronze," Tommy had agreed.

Gold meant three nights, extra sessions, and another hundred dollars a month they didn't have.

Now, as they followed Rick into the main cage area, she tried not to do the math. Two nights a week. Eight weeks. Sixteen trips up and down the highway. Gas. Time. Sandwiches eaten in parking lots.

Homework done in the back seat. All of it for something that used to be called winter and used to mean rest.

"Parents can watch from up top," Rick said, pointing to a metal staircase that led to a narrow balcony. "We've got tables, a coffee setup, even a payphone if you need to call out. We just ask that you let our staff handle instruction. No sideline coaching, please."

He smiled as he said it, like a man who'd had that fight before. "Boys, grab a band and get in lines by height," he called. "Let's get loose."

Tyler and Kyle moved toward a bin of resistance bands, falling in with a loose crowd of boys in hoodies and shorts. Some wore Elite gear head to toe. Others had their high school logos half-hidden under navy pullovers.

"Lines by height," Kyle muttered. "Guess I'm in the hobbit group."
"Shut up," Tyler said, grinning anyway.

Up on the balcony, Tommy and Karyn took seats at the rail, looking down through the netting at the organized chaos. Parents filled the row: laptops open, notebooks out, the occasional video camera propped on a tripod. The glow from their screens reflected off the plexiglass, making the cages below look like a game on TV with the sound turned down.

"You want anything?" Tommy asked. "They've got coffee." "I'm good," Karyn said. Her eyes never left the boys.

Reps and Waiting

The winter-cage routine found its rhythm fast. Bands and dynamic stretches. Throwing progressions down the "long toss" lane, which was long mostly in the brochure. Then stations: tee work, front toss, short rounds in the cage with a coach feeding balls from behind L-screens.

"Five swings and switch," one coach barked. "Move with urgency, fellas. We're getting our work in."

Tyler would step in, put a handful of good swings on the ball, and then step out for five, ten, fifteen minutes of waiting while everyone else did the same. The math didn't favor hitters. This was a place where the word reps sounded big and the reality came in brief bursts surrounded by standing still.

Upstairs, Karyn watched Tyler lean against the cage rail, bat tucked under his arm, eyes following the batter three kids ahead. Kyle stood in a catching lane, dropping to his knees again and again as balls bounced off the matting in front of him.

She pulled out a small notebook and wrote without looking away. Winter Performance — eight weeks. Cost: $1,060. Actual swings: ? Further down: Boys home after 9 p.m. Homework: ?

She closed the notebook, but the numbers stayed open in her mind.

An Old Coach in a New Building By the third week, Jack knew he couldn't just listen to stories about the Academy from the bleachers at Veterans. If he was going to understand the world the boys were being pulled into, he had to walk into it.

The invitation came at the donut shop.

"Coach Thompson," Rick said, spotting him in line. "We'd love to have you take a look at what we're doing. Maybe talk to the boys about the mental side. Bring that old-school wisdom into a modern setup, you know?"

Jack hesitated. The last indoor place he'd worked in had turned into a pipeline for kids who never learned how to love a bad hop.

But the Ruggiero boys were in the winter group. So were half a dozen kids he'd watched grow from T-ball to middle school. If they were going to be in that building, he needed to see it with his own eyes.

That Tuesday he walked through the Academy door with his hands in his coat pockets, understanding the words on the walls but not the system underneath them.

Rick met him in the lobby with a handshake that tried to sell three things at once: authority, friendliness, and shared history.

"Coach Thompson," he said, using the title like a compliment. "Appreciate you coming down. Boys!" he called, raising his voice. "We've got a special guest tonight. Some of you work with Coach Jack over at Veterans. He's forgotten more about this game than most guys ever learn."

Jack winced inwardly at the line but kept his face calm. From the field level, the cages looked even smaller. Nets hung from ceiling to turf. Balls clattered off screens, the sound swallowed and fed back by metal walls. Kids in hoodies moved station to station, figures in a system rather than on a field.

When it was bullpen time, Rick steered him toward the lane where Tyler and three other pitchers were getting loose.

"Why don't you stand back here with me," Rick said, stopping behind the mound. "See what you think."

Tyler saw Jack and straightened, the way a kid does when an adult he respects has slipped into the room.

"Just throw," Jack told him. "Don't throw for me."

Tyler's first few pitches were solid — downhill, around the mitt. The bullpen coach stood off to the side with a clipboard and a handheld gun. Each throw came with a number and a note.

"Seventy-four. Good. Stay tall. Seventy-five. Better. Ride that slope. Seventy-three. Don't baby it — we can handle twenty more."

Jack watched the boy's shoulders as much as he watched the ball. They rose and tightened with every number called out.

When Tyler stepped aside, the next kid climbed the mound already chasing someone else's reading.

After the pitchers finished, Rick gathered the entire group into a half circle at the back of the main cage.

"Alright, fellas, eyes up," he said. "We talk a lot here about metrics, about velocity and exit velo and all that. Tonight I want you to hear from someone who's seen the whole pipeline. Coach Jack, you want to give them a few words?"

He stepped back, ceding the floor. Jack moved to the middle of the arc and took his cap off. It felt wrong to address players with his head covered, even under a roof.

"You all look tired," he said. A few boys laughed. He let the sound settle. "That's not a criticism. Tired's part of it."

He let his gaze rest on Tyler for a heartbeat, then drift on.

"These cages are tools. So are weighted balls, bands, all the gadgets. Tools are good if you use them right. They're not magic. Being here isn't the same as getting better."

He held the room a moment longer than was comfortable. "Use this place," he said finally. "Don't let it own you."

There was a beat of silence. Then one of the younger kids clapped. Another joined him. The rest followed, the sound a little unsure, like they weren't sure whether this counted as part of the program.

"Exactly," Rick said, stepping forward again with an easy grin. "That's why we marry that old-school grit to modern data. We use every tool to give you an edge. Alright, grab water. Back to work."

As the boys scattered, Tyler passed close enough to Jack for a quick exchange.

"You mean it?" he asked quietly. "About it not owning us?"

"Every word," Jack said.

The Wear

The weeks blurred. Drive up. Bands. Throws. Stations. Drive home. Tyler's elbow didn't hurt, exactly, but the stiffness now took longer to shake out each night. He mentioned it once to Rick.

"Add a few more band sets and make sure you're getting your recovery work in," Rick said. "That's what makes the difference."

Kyle's knees complained on the ride home after nights heavy on blocking drills. He learned to angle the heater vents toward his legs and flex his toes so the joints didn't lock up.

Tommy noticed how both boys sank deeper into the couch on offnights, homework sheets glowing in front of tired eyes. The chatter they used to bring home from pickup games—who'd made a diving catch, who'd hit a ball into the creek—had been replaced by shorter reports.

"How was it?" "Fine." One night, after they'd gone to bed, Tommy stood in the kitchen doorway and said what had been sitting in his chest for three weeks. "We can pull them out," he told Karyn. "Tell Rick it's too much. Nobody can make us stay."

Karyn leaned against the counter, notebook closed under her hand. "And tell the boys what?" she asked. "That we quit in the middle? That we wasted the money? Half these parents think if you're not here you're not serious."

"I don't care what half these parents think," Tommy said, but he did care about what those opinions did to his sons.

She opened the notebook and ran her finger down the columns. "Two weeks left," she said. "Let's get through it. Then we sit down with Jack and the boys and figure out a better plan for spring."

Tommy exhaled. "Okay," he said. "Two weeks." She added another line.

Winter Performance—Weeks 1–6: Cost: $795. Boys' faces after practice: getting duller.

A Door and a Sky

On the last night of the program, a late-season storm rolled in. Snow hammered the metal roof in hard, slanting sheets. Cars fishtailed a little in the lot before finding their spots. Inside, the air felt even drier than usual, the fluorescent buzz a touch louder.

Halfway through the session, the cages went dark.

The lights flickered once, twice, then cut out completely. For a heartbeat, everything stopped. No clank of balls. No coaches barking. No hum of fans. Just the sound of wind against the walls and a dozen kids' breaths caught in the dark. Emergency lights blinked on over the exit doors, throwing dim red pools along the floor. "Everybody stay where you are," a coach called. "We're fine. Just a power blip."

Phones lit up the balcony as parents called home or pulled up the local TV station's site on the laptops they'd brought to the cages. The radar bands were rolling straight over the North Shore.

Down on the turf, Tyler and Kyle stood side by side, hands on their knees, waiting for someone to tell them what to do next.

Rick gathered the staff near the office door. There was a lot of gesturing, a lot of shrugged shoulders. Ten minutes passed. The main lights stayed dead.

"Alright," he announced finally, voice echoing weirdly in the half-dark. "We're going to call it for tonight. We'll add an extra session next week for the guys who can make it. Players, grab your gear and head out with your parents. Be careful in the lot."

The boys moved toward the exits in a slow, shuffling pack. Jackets were pulled on over damp T-shirts. Cleats clicked on concrete.

Tyler reached the door first and yanked it open. The cold hit his face like a bucket of water.

"Feels good," he said. "I forgot what real air feels like." Kyle stuck his tongue out, catching a snowflake. "Tastes better too," he said.

They slogged through the slush to the car, breath sharp in the wind. For the first time in weeks, neither of them was in a rush to talk about radar readings or "velo jumps."

Tommy started the engine, wipers scraping at the windshield. The defroster wheezed to life.

"You know," he said, easing the car onto the slick road, "when I was your age, winter meant shoveling the driveway and seeing how far we could throw a ball in boots. That was our performance program."

Tyler watched the ghost-white fields slide past outside his window. "Times change," he said.

"Yeah," Tommy answered. "They do." But as they drove past the barely visible outline of Cedarbrook Field— just a darker rectangle under the snow—he felt something in him tighten against the idea that this was the only way forward.

In his coat pocket, folded and worn from weeks of handling, the winter-program contract crinkled softly every time he turned the wheel.

Back at his small kitchen table later that night, Jack unfolded the Academy flyer and laid it beside an old photo of Cedarbrook Field in winter — kids in heavy coats shoveling a path from home to first, breath visible, cheeks red.

He looked from the picture to the pamphlet and back again.

He picked up a pen and wrote three words across the bottom of the flyer before tossing it into the trash.

Remember the sky.

Outside, the storm howled over the marsh. Inside, boys slept in small rooms, arms sore, calendars full. Somewhere under the noise, the game they'd fallen in love with was still waiting, intact.

Chapter Six — Carpool Years

,

2003 · Chestnut Street to Everywhere Else

HOMEWORK IN THE BACK seat, gas receipts in the glove compartment. By the time the calendar on the Ruggiero fridge said 2003, their life could be measured in miles. The miles from Chestnut Street to the middle school.

From the middle school to the Academy. From the Academy to whatever weekend complex the schedule dictated. On nights when the minivan's dashboard glowed a tired green and the radio hummed low to keep everyone awake, Tommy sometimes imagined their route traced in permanent marker across a map of the North Shore—tight loops and long stretches radiating out from two points.

Cedarbrook Field.

And the Academy.

The boys' shoes lived by the door in an untidy heap. Their bags never really got unpacked, just refilled. The kitchen table belonged to the schedule: printed grids from North Shore Elite, high school game slates, Karyn's handwritten notes in the margins.

Ty – practice 5:30–7:30 (NSE) Ky – practice 6:00–7:30 (middle school) Jack @ Veterans – Sat a. m. (try to get them there) Gas $? The question marks multiplied faster than the miles.

After-School Routes

Most weekdays, the carpool started the same way. "Drop Tyler first," Kyle would say, sliding into the back seat with his backpack half-zipped. "He's got to be early."

Tyler would protest, just enough to sound polite. "No, it's fine, we can—" "Kyle," Karyn would cut in. "You have homework club on Tuesdays. Tyler, you have to be there before the coaches. We're not debating it every week."

So they'd do the loop. House to school.

School to Academy. Academy back to school or home, depending on the day. Back to Academy.

Then home again. Some afternoons, the van filled with extra boys—Marco from down the street, Moose from the next town over whose parents both worked nights. Cleats banged against the floor. The air turned thick with sweat, grass, and cafeteria pizza.

Homework happened wherever it could. Homework followed them everywhere that year: at the kitchen table while Karyn packed sandwiches, on the Academy bleachers under bad fluorescent light, most often in the back seat with cleats knocking against algebra books.

Kyle tried to brace his notebook against his knees, writing between bumps, a strange little rhythm that left his pages full of jagged lines and half-formed letters.

"Show your work," his teacher would scribble in the margins. I did, he wanted to write back. You just couldn't see what the road did to it.

Tyler read social studies chapters by the passing glow of streetlights. On nights when they hit every red light, he'd get through another page. On nights when traffic flowed, he fell behind. "Don't worry," Tommy would say. "You'll catch up when we get there."

They never quite said whether he meant school or baseball. Glove Compartment Ledger The glove compartment took the brunt of it. Gas receipts stuffed in hastily. Tournament parking stubs. Crumpled concession slips. Karyn's handwriting on the backs of envelopes: $35 – cages $25 – extra lesson $12 – tolls One night, killing time while practice ran long, Tommy opened it to look for a registration packet and the whole paper nest spilled onto the passenger floor.

"Sorry," Karyn said. "I meant to clean that out." Tommy bent to gather them, flattening each slip against his thigh before stacking it on the console. It looked like nothing. Small numbers. Bits of ink.

But as he spread them out, a picture formed. "Gas alone..." he murmured. "This month..." "Don't," Karyn said, eyes on the field through the windshield. "If you add it up all at once, I'll throw up."

He added anyway, quietly, with a stub of pencil he found under the seat. When he stopped, his stomach turned.

He flipped one receipt over and wrote a note to himself. Don't show Tyler this.

He wasn't ashamed of the cost. It wasn't that. He just didn't want his son standing on a mound somewhere thinking, That pitch is worth eighty-four dollars and twenty cents. The game already asked enough of a kid's heart. It didn't need to charge interest.

He stuffed the receipts back into the compartment, less neatly than before. The door wouldn't quite shut all the way. It hung open a crack, papers visible like a throat trying to swallow too much at once.

Small Conversations, Big Questions On Fridays, when the week had ground them down to dull edges, the car felt more like a confession booth than a vehicle.

"Coach says we should start thinking about showcases," Tyler said once, forehead leaning against the cool window, watching a billboard for a casino slide past. "He says the best guys my age are already on college radars."

"How old are those radars?" Kyle asked from the back, deadpan. "Shut up, Ky," Tyler muttered, but the corner of his mouth twitched. "What did Coach say exactly?" Tommy asked.

"He said if we don't get to at least one big event this summer, we'll be behind guys in Jersey and Florida and out west," Tyler answered. "He says scouts live at those places now."

Tommy's jaw worked. "And how do you feel about that?" he asked. Tyler shrugged. "I don't know. I just don't want to be the kid who didn't go and then finds out that's why he didn't get looked at."

Karyn watched his reflection in the rearview mirror.

"Do you want to go," she asked, "or do you just not want to be the only one who doesn't?"

Tyler considered that for longer than anyone expected. "Both?" he said. "I like competing. I like big fields. But it's like... every time we say yes to something, I can feel the no somewhere else. To Nana's. To church. To just being home."

The wipers squeaked over dry glass. The radio murmured about traffic three towns away.

"We'll do some," Tommy said. "We're not going to chase every whistle that blows. But we'll pick our spots."

"And if that's the difference between me playing in college or not?" Tyler pressed.

"Then it was never really the difference," Tommy said, more sure in that moment than he felt. "The coaches who matter won't need you in every brochure to see you."

Kyle stared at the back of his father's head. He filed the sentence away.

Saturdays at Veterans

The carpool years weren't all highway. Jack made sure of that.

Most Saturdays, as long as the weather cooperated and the calendar hadn't already claimed every hour, he opened Veterans Field for whoever could get there. No sign-up. No fee. No banners.

Just a time. "Ten o'clock," he'd say in passing during the week. "Come late if you have to. Leave early if you must. Just show up for an hour if you can."

The first few months, the crowd was small—six or seven kids in mismatched hats and hoodies. By the time word filtered through schools and text messages, a dozen or more showed up regularly.

The Ruggieros tried to make it more often than not. Some Saturdays, Tyler had to choose between an extra "optional" session at the Academy and Jack's free work. Sometimes— much to Coach Rick's mild annoyance—he chose the fence.

"Live reps matter," Jack would say when Ty jogged in from the lot, slightly out of breath. "Let's use them."

They ran ground-ball circuits that left thighs burning and backs damp. They worked on footwork around the bag, on turns at second that had more to do with balance than flair. They practiced communication on pop-ups in the twilight, voices cutting through the cold.

"Yours!" "Mine!" "Nobody's—let it go." Jack wove small conversations into the drills, one or two sentences at a time. Be the kid who picks up other people's helmets. That kid always gets invited back.

Kyle soaked it up. So did a handful of other boys whose names Jack stored carefully in the ledger of his memory.

Tommy liked those mornings because they didn't involve the glove compartment ledger. Veterans cost time and gas. That was it.

One Saturday, as the boys ran a relay drill from foul pole to foul pole, he and Karyn sat on the bleachers with paper cups of coffee that had gone lukewarm in the breeze.

"I like it here," Karyn said. "Better coffee?" Tommy asked. "Worse coffee," she said, smiling. "Better everything else."

Down on the field, Tyler and Marco sprinted neck-and-neck, laughing, neither in a numbered shirt.

Calendar Wall

The schedule eventually grew too big for the fridge. One Sunday night, Karyn cleared a section of the hallway wall and taped up a fresh month from a big-box office store calendar. Around it, she arranged practice grids, tournament flyers, game slates, and work shifts.

Monday: Ty – Academy; Ky – school practice Tuesday: Ty – high school; Ky – off (homework) Wednesday: Ty – Academy; Ky – Veterans if weather Thursday: Ty – off; Ky – Academy catching clinic Friday: High school scrimmage Sat– Sun: Tournament (if seeded) "This is insane," she said flatly, magnet in hand. "We're insane." "Everybody else is doing it," Tyler said, more out of habit than conviction.

"Everybody else also thinks their kid's going to Vanderbilt," Karyn replied. "News flash, there aren't that many spots."

She regretted the sharpness as soon as it left her mouth, but the air had already shifted.

Tyler's jaw set. "I didn't ask to do all of this," he said quietly. "You're the ones who signed me up. You're the ones driving."

Karyn opened her mouth, then closed it again. Tommy stepped in. "He's not wrong," he said. "We're in this, too." They stood in the small rectangle of kitchen light like three sides of a triangle, each trying to see the others' point, each tired enough to fail.

Later that night, after the boys had gone to bed and the house had settled, Tommy opened the notebook again.

He added a new heading. Non-money cost: Underneath, in small, cramped letters, he wrote: Missed dinners. Missed sleep. Missed time with Nana. Missed church. Missed just being bored.

He didn't show that page to anyone. Another Kind of Carpool Whenever he could, Jack tried to steal the boys from the minivan. If he was headed past Chestnut Street on his way to Veterans, he'd swing into their driveway and give a quick honk or a wave.

"Hop in," he'd say. "I'm going down anyway." The boys loved riding with him. The truck smelled like coffee and pine and sawdust. The radio was set to the AM station that still did game recaps and call-in shows with people who called pitchers "hurlers" and thought pitch counts were for the weak.

Jack drove slower than Tommy, but the conversations were richer.

"You know what I remember about my carpool years?" he asked one afternoon as Tyler and Kyle sat side by side, knees almost touching the dashboard because the seat wouldn't slide back any farther.

"What?" Tyler said. "Nothing," Jack replied. "That's the thing. I remember fields. I remember plays. I remember who sat next to me on the bench. I barely remember the rides. They all blended. So don't let the car become the story. Let it just be the road."

Kyle looked out the window at the long line of headlights in front of them. "What if it already feels like the story?" he asked.

"Then you notice it," Jack said. "You talk about it with the people you're in the car with. And you make sure it isn't the only story you're writing."

He tapped the steering wheel as they merged onto the highway. After a minute he added, almost to himself: "Lady I knew once kept a notebook for things like that. Everything she didn't want the road to swallow."

"Who?" Kyle asked.

"Friend of mine," Jack said. "Long time ago. You'd have liked her."

He didn't say anything else for a while.

One Small Rebellion

The carpool years rolled on until one evening, almost by accident, the Ruggieros did something quietly rebellious.

It was a Thursday. The plan on the fridge said: Ty – Academy (hitting) Ky – Academy (defense) At four-thirty, the sky opened up. Not a snowstorm this time, but a cold, miserable rain that made the world look like it was behind a dirty window.

Tommy came in from work, shaking water from his jacket. Karyn stood at the sink, staring out through the streaked glass at the street.

"The roads are going to be a mess," he said. "But we can make it if we leave now." He said it automatically, muscle memory of a man who'd beaten traffic for years. Karyn didn't move.

"Call it," she said. "What?" "Call it," she repeated. "For once, let's be the family that doesn't drive forty minutes in this to stand in a cage under fluorescent lights."

He hesitated. "Rick will say—" "I know exactly what Rick will say," Karyn cut in. "He'll say consistency, commitment, windows, opportunity. He'll say all the words he always says. But I'm looking at our boys falling asleep on top of unfinished homework, and I'm looking at that wall calendar, and I'm thinking... we're allowed to say no. Just once."

Tommy studied her face, the tired set of her shoulders. "Okay," he said finally. "I'll call it."

He stepped into the hallway and dialed. "Hey, Rick," he said when the coach answered. "It's Tommy Ruggiero. Listen, the weather's junk and the boys are beat. We're going to stay local tonight. See you this weekend."

Rick launched into a polished speech about consistency and opportunity. Tommy listened, then calmly repeated himself.

"We'll be there this weekend," he said. "We're just not going to die on Route 1 for a Thursday hitting session."

He hung up before he could talk himself out of it. When he told the boys, Tyler looked surprised.

"We're... not going?" he asked, like the words might break if he said them wrong.

"Not tonight," Tommy said. "Jack's going to open Veterans for anyone who wants it. If the rain lets up, we'll go down there. If it doesn't, we'll play cards and you can finish your homework before midnight for once."

Kyle lifted both hands in mock celebration. "I vote cards either way," he said.

The rain eased to a mist around six. At six-thirty, the Ruggieros pulled into the Veterans lot instead of the highway on-ramp.

Only three other cars were there. The field was soft but playable. The fence glistened with tiny beads of water. Jack stood near home in a raincoat, cap pulled low.

"Thought you'd be at the cages," he said as they walked up. "Not tonight," Tommy replied. "We exercised our right to be human." Jack's grin was quick and genuine.

"Good," he said. "Field's been lonely."

They played a loose three-on-three with ghost runners and self--umpiring until the light fell out of the sky. By the time they walked back to the car, everyone was soaked to the shins and splotched with mud.

On the walk back, Tyler fell in step beside his father. "Coach is gonna be mad, isn't he?" he asked. "Probably," Tommy said. "You okay with that?" Tyler thought for a moment, then nodded. "Yeah," he said. "Tonight was worth it."

In years to come, that night would stand in Jack's mind for the wet grass and the laughter and the small mutiny of having stayed.

Chapter Seven — Ranking Season

,

THE FIRST LIST DIDN'T arrive in an envelope or on letterhead. It came home as a printed email, folded in half and slapped under the fridge magnet that usually held the week's schedule. Across the top margin, in Kyle's crooked handwriting, someone had written: Ty Top 100? ...and drawn a lopsided smiley face. The paper itself was grainy black--and-white, the logo at the top a little blurred from low printer toner. Underneath, columns of names marched down the page.

NORTHEAST 14U PROSPECT RANKINGS—MIDSEASON UPDATE

There were headings: Overall Top 100, Position Rankings, Risers to Watch. Each line had a name, town, position, guessed-at height and weight, and a row of stars. A number sat beside each entry, reducing each kid to a slot on a chart.

Tommy leaned against the counter with his work jacket still on and read down the list. He saw familiar town names first— Peabody, Lynn, Revere, Saugus. Then familiar program names, including North Shore Elite, stamped like a watermark next to a third of the entries.

The back door squeaked. Tyler walked in, still in his school clothes, backpack hanging from one shoulder.

"What's that?" he asked. "Mail," Tommy said. "The kind we didn't used to get."

He handed the paper over. Tyler's eyes ran down the page, lips moving slightly. He saw names he knew—kids he'd played with, against, or heard about in dugouts and on car rides. A boy from Connecticut at #1.

A tall lefty from New Hampshire at #5. Marco at #62 with a tiny "2" and a note in italics: projectable arm, needs polish.

Then his own name. Ruggiero, Tyler. Something tightened in his chest. It wasn't quite pride and it wasn't quite fear. It was both, stacked on top of each other.

"Three stars," Kyle said from the doorway, peering over his shoulder. "That's pretty good, right? Like... out of three?"

The joke landed only halfway. "How many stars are there?" Tyler asked. Tommy shrugged. "When I was your age, we had box scores in the paper. You were either in there or you weren't. No constellations attached."

"Four," Kyle said. "Coach Rick showed us their site. Three is 'strong regional prospect.' Four is 'national potential.' " Tyler's eyes lingered on that last phrase—national potential. "What's 'no stars'?" he asked. Kyle's smile thinned. "Invisible, I guess." He flipped to the positional lists— shortstop, right-handed pitcher. Found his name again, lower than he wanted on both.

He didn't see Kyle's name anywhere. The paper suddenly felt heavier in his hand. He set it back on the counter like it might dent the laminate.

Screens and Scores

The list came from a site called ProspectMap, one of half a dozen that had sprung up in the short blink between dial-up and high-speed.

They had slick logos and aggressive taglines: We see tomorrow's stars today. Where the next level comes to find you.

Parents and kids built profiles—height, weight, school, GPA, tournament stats. They uploaded video, paid for "enhanced visibility," and checked who had "viewed" their pages.

North Shore Elite had a partnership with two of the sites. "Part of the value we offer your family," Coach Rick told them at a preseason parent meeting, "is access to these platforms. Our players are automatically entered into their ranking pools. They come to our events. They use our data. It's a win-win."

The words data and platform had somehow become normal in sentences about fourteen-year-olds.

On team nights, the balcony at the Academy glowed not just with field lights, but with laptop screens. Parents scrolled through rankings while their kids hit in the cages below.

"Look, he bumped from fifty-four to forty-one after that last showcase." "Coach says if we get him into two more events, he'll get on the risers list." "Did you see they added a 'commitment meter' to their profiles now?"

Tyler pretended not to care at first. He told himself it was just noise. But one afternoon, the Academy computers were free between hitting groups, and curiosity slid past whatever pride he had left.

He typed his name into the search bar. His profile came up with a headshot Coach Rick had snapped at last summer's camp. The bio underneath had obviously been written in the Academy office.

Tyler Ruggiero - RHP/SS - North Shore Elite. Three-star prospect. Strong regional follow. Clean arm action, projectable frame. Competes well. Needs to refine secondary stuff and add strength.

Polished. Projectable. Needs. He noticed what wasn't there.

No mention of how he settled pitchers down between innings. Nothing about the way he owned a bad at-bat, or the way he took extra grounders at the end of practice without being asked.

Just the measurable. He clicked over to the Overall Rankings. Scrolled to #37.

Ruggiero, Tyler—N. S. Elite.

He stared at the names above and below his. Dots in some new sky. He wondered what the kid at #12 looked like. Wondered if he was really that much better. Wondered if scouts already knew his name.

The floorboard creaked behind him. Without thinking, Tyler jabbed the power button and blacked the screen out.

"Don't," Karyn said from the doorway. "Don't what?" he asked. "Don't hide it," she said. "You're allowed to look."

She stepped into the spill of light from the lamp, folding her arms. "Is it... bad?" Tyler asked. "Being thirty-seven? Being three stars?" She took a breath, choosing her words.

"It's information," she said. "Not truth. Truth is how you play and how you act. Lists are just snapshots."

"A snapshot everyone can see," Tyler muttered. She laid a hand on the back of his chair.

"You know what I see when I look at you?" she asked. He didn't answer. "I see a kid who works hard," she said. "Who makes other kids better. Who does homework in the car and still finds time to make his little cousin laugh at family parties. I see a good son and a good brother."

He rolled his eyes, but only halfway. "That's not what college coaches are looking at," he said. "Some of the good ones are," she replied. "The rest... I'm not sure we want you playing for them."

He stared at the blank monitor. "What if I'm not on there next year?" he asked, letting the real fear out. "What if I drop?"

"Then we print it and use it to start the grill," she said. "You're not a stock, Ty. We didn't buy shares of you."

He snorted.

"Feels like everybody else did," he said. She squeezed his shoulder.

"Eat your dinner," she said. "The screen will still be there in the morning. So will the field."

Dinner Table Numbers

The list slid into the rest of their life. Tyler started recognizing names from ProspectMap in dugouts: That kid's #18, that pitcher's a four-star, that catcher's "under-the-radar." He felt it seeping into conversations, into how kids lined up, into who took extra batting practice and who quietly drifted to the back of the cage.

At home, the topic floated across the table whether they wanted it to or not.

"Coach thinks if I get on the risers list, more schools will see my profile," Tyler said one night between forkfuls of pasta. "He says they check it every week."

"Do you want to be on it?" Tommy asked. "I... guess," Tyler said. "Doesn't everyone?"

Kyle twirled spaghetti around his fork, eyes on his plate. "You don't have to live on that site," Karyn said. "It's not the Bible." "It's what everyone talks about," Tyler replied. "If I'm not on it, it's like I don't exist."

Kyle let his fork clink down, a little louder than he meant to. "I don't exist there at all," he said, trying for light and missing. The quiet that followed was small, but sharp.

Tommy looked between them. "Hey," he said. "I've been around this game long enough to tell you: a lot of kids who never sniff a ranking sheet end up having pretty good careers. And some of the ones on page one disappear as soon as the lights get a little brighter."

Tyler picked at his pasta and didn't answer. Kyle picked his fork back up.

Jack and the Paper

The first time Jack saw Tyler's name in print, it was on the back page of a convenience store newspaper, below the lottery numbers and above the classifieds.

He'd stopped for coffee. The headline on the sports page had nothing to do with Saugus—some college football story out west— but a little box on the side of the page caught his eye: ProspectMap Northeast—Top 50 14U Prospects (see full list online) He scanned the names. There it was: Ruggiero, Tyler – #37. "Your boy made the list," the cashier said, following his gaze. "Coach Rick was in here talking about it. Big deal, right?"

Jack grunted something noncommittal, paid for his coffee, and carried the paper out into the cold.

He read the list once in the truck, then flipped to the real reason he still bought a paper at all—the box scores.

Saugus 4, Peabody 3.

Lynn English 7, Salem 2. Under each line: a handful of names. 2-for3, RBI. 6 IP, 3 H, 2 ER. Facts. No stars.

He thought about the kids in those lines, some of whom would never appear on any regional prospect list. He thought about the way college coaches used to call: quiet, direct, human. Tell me about this kid.

They didn't ask for stars. They asked for stories. That afternoon at Veterans, Tyler showed up early, list already folded in his back pocket, the crease worn from being pulled out and put away more than he wanted to admit.

"Coach," he said, handing Jack the paper, "did you see this?" Jack glanced at the column, then at Tyler.

"What do you think of it?" he asked. Tyler hesitated.

"I think... it's kinda cool," he said. "And I think... now if I mess up, they'll say I didn't deserve it."

Jack folded the page in half. "That's pretty honest," he said.

"Coach Rick says it proves I'm on the right track," Tyler added. "That schools will start to notice."

Jack walked a few steps toward shortstop and planted his boots in the dirt. "There's something you need to know about lists like this," he said. "They're not evil. They're not holy. They're business. They live off attention."

Tyler frowned. "So they don't matter?" he asked. Jack shook his head.

"They matter a little," he said. "Some coaches glance at them. Then they call people like me and say, 'Is this kid what they say he is?' My answer doesn't come from a website. It comes from watching you here."

He tapped the dirt with the toe of his boot. "Here is where you make your case," he said. "Not online." Tyler nodded slowly.

"Okay," he said. "Good," Jack replied. "Now do that footwork drill again. Your right foot's getting lazy on backhands. I don't care what ProspectMap thinks of your exit velo if you're letting balls eat you up in the six-hole."

The sting of the words was softened by the half-smile at the corner of his mouth.

They went back to work. When Jack got home, he dropped the newspaper in the trash and wrote a short line in his ledger.

Ty – handles list with honesty. Good sign. Whispered Labels The rankings did something more dangerous than put numbers beside names. They created labels.

"Top-50 kid," someone would say about a boy from another town. "Borderline prospect," about another.

"Under-the-radar," which usually meant, we haven't decided if he's worth chasing yet.

Parents used the phrases in the stands like new vocabulary from a seminar. Karyn heard it one afternoon during a high school scrimmage.

"Who's that at short?" a mother from another town asked. "The one who made the backhand play."

"That's the Ruggiero boy," another replied. "He's a three-star on ProspectMap. Good player. Coach Rick says he's got projectable tools." "What about the catcher?" "Oh, that's his little brother. I don't think he's on the radar yet." On the radar.

The phrase scraped across her nerves. As if somewhere there was a screen making green circles over acceptable children and leaving the rest in blank space.

Later, in the car, she asked. "Do you guys hear that kind of talk?" she said. "Stars. Radar. Top-this, under-that?" Tyler shrugged. "Sometimes," he said. "Usually from parents."

Kyle stared out the window. "Guys on my team talk about it too," he said quietly. "Like, 'He's a four-star,' or, 'He's not on any list.' " "What do they say about you?" Karyn asked. Kyle gave a half-laugh.

"They don't," he said. "Feels like being the scoreboard when it's turned off."

Tyler looked over at him. "You're my four-star catcher," he said. Kyle rolled his eyes. "Shut up and throw," he said. But the smile that crept in afterward was cleaner than anything the ranking season had given him.

The lists didn't vanish. ProspectMap kept updating. Parents kept checking. The Academy kept forwarding "updated evaluations" with soft nudges toward more events.

But something shifted in the Ruggieros' house—and at Veterans. They still saw the numbers.

They just stopped pretending those were the only ones that counted.

RANKINGS RELEASE DAY—AFTER SCHOOL

The list went live at 3:02 p.m., and by 3:06 it had become the only thing anyone could talk about.

It wasn't official. Just a glossy website with a donation button and a list of names arranged to look inevitable. In the cages boys checked their phones between swings. Coaches pretended not to notice, which was its own kind of noticing.

Tyler didn't check. Not at first. He told himself he didn't need it. He told himself the game was real and the internet was wind.

Then he heard a laugh—sharp, delighted—and turned to see a boy holding up a screen. "I'm top twenty," the boy said, letting the words hang there.

Coach Carver walked in with his clipboard and his grin. "All right," he said, tapping the paper, "we've got some visibility now. That changes expectations."

He called names and sent boys to stations. When he got to Tyler, he paused, the pause doing its own work.

"Tyler," he said. "You're on tees today." Tee work was for kids who needed fixing. Or kids you wanted to remind of their place.

Tyler held his bat and felt the heat climb his neck. He swallowed it down. He went to the tee. He did what he always did: worked.

A phone buzzed in his pocket. He looked despite himself. Not listed.

Not in the top fifty. Not in the honorable mentions. Nothing. For a second, the cage noise fell away. The sound that stayed was his own heartbeat—fast, embarrassed, loud.

Coach Carver approached as if he'd been waiting. "These lists," he murmured, "are about exposure. But exposure can be earned."

He handed Tyler a card.

PRIVATE EVALUATION. LIMITED SLOTS.

"Come in early," the coach said. "We can get you seen. We can get you on paper."

Tyler stared at the card. The offer helped and insulted him at the same time. He nodded because he didn't know what else to do.

That night, in his room, he taped the card to the wall above his desk. Not as a gift. As a dare.

He sat on the edge of his bed and looked at it for a while. He had not taped anything to that wall since the Pedro Martinez glossy that had come folded in a baseball card pack when he was eight, the one whose corners he had pressed flat with his thumb every morning that summer because he couldn't stand to see them curling. The Pedro had come down a few years ago. The new tack was still in the wall, a little crooked.

He thought about the kid who had said I'm top twenty in the cage that afternoon. He thought about how easy it had been for the cage to go quiet around the kid's sentence and how loud it had been around his own pocket when his phone buzzed not listed. He tried to make himself feel angry. The anger came easier than the other thing — the other thing being a kind of small dropping feeling he didn't have a word for, a feeling like missing a step in the dark.

His shoulder ached from the day's swings, but he stood up and swung in the mirror anyway, slow and angry, shaping his body into what the list demanded.

Downstairs, Tommy heard the thud of the bat against air and didn't go up.

Chapter Eight — The Injury

The first time

Kyle's elbow really hurt, he didn't tell anyone. By Tuesday night his legs had stopped belonging to him. He'd caught four innings for the middle school, then six more under metal rafters for North Shore Elite because the older team's catcher was "dinged up," which was adult language for somebody else's boy can absorb this one.

"You can handle it," Rick had said, tossing him the gear. "You're durable. Guys like you play a long time."

Durable. It sounded like a compliment. It felt like a sentence. By the last inning, every throw back to the mound sent a small spark through the underside of his elbow. Not enough to drop him. Enough to make him want to rub at it when no one was looking.

He didn't. Tough kids didn't complain. Catchers especially. So he finished the game, shook hands in the line, stuffed his gear in his bag, and climbed into the back seat with his hoodie pulled over his head.

"You okay?" Tommy asked in the rearview as they pulled onto Route 1. "I'm fine," Kyle said. "Just tired."

He said it again two nights later, when they added another seven innings to the tally. By the end of the week, tired had turned into something else.

Ice and Silence

The Ruggiero freezer had always been full of ice packs—auras of blue and white shoved between frozen peas and stray popsicles. This year, they lived mostly on the kitchen table.

"Fifteen minutes on, fifteen off," Karyn would say, sliding one toward Tyler after a long outing. "Don't argue. I do this for a living."

One night, after a doubleheader, she noticed something different. Tyler's arm was bare. Kyle's wasn't.

He sat at the table with his right elbow wrapped in a dish towel, an ice pack balanced on top, his homework pushed just out of drip range.

"Trade with your brother?" she asked lightly. Kyle shrugged. "My knees feel fine tonight," he said. "Just figured I'd get ahead on the arm." He tried to smile. It didn't quite get there.

"How long has it bugged you?" she asked. "Couple days," he said. "It's nothing."

She reached out and peeled the towel back. His elbow looked normal—no angry swelling, no purple streaks. But when she pressed gently along the inside, just above the bone, he flinched before he could stop himself.

"That hurts?" she asked. "It's fine," he said. "That's not what I asked." He shifted in his chair, eyes on his worksheet.

"It's just sore," he muttered. "Rick says that's part of the position. You get used to it." Karyn's jaw tightened. "Rick doesn't sleep in your arm," she said. "You do."

Tommy came in from the living room, catching the tail end. "What's up?" he asked.

"Kyle's elbow," Karyn said. "He says it's sore." Tommy frowned. "How sore?" he asked. "Three out of ten," Kyle said automatically.

"On a normal human scale?" Karyn asked. "Or on the 'I don't want to miss games' scale?" "On the 'everyone else plays through stuff' scale," Kyle said.

Tommy and Karyn exchanged a look. "Let me see your schedule," Tommy said.

Kyle slid his backpack over with his left hand. Tommy dug out the crumpled practice grid and game list.

Middle school: four games this week. Academy: three practices, one scrimmage. Weekend: tournament "weather permitting."

"That's where your pain is coming from," Tommy said quietly. Kyle stared at the table.

"I can handle it," he said. "Ty throws way more than I do. He's fine." "That's not how bodies work," Karyn said. "Pain isn't a contest."

He pulled the towel back over his elbow, shutting the conversation down. "I have a game tomorrow," he said. "Can we talk about it next week?" They didn't.

The machine didn't leave room on the calendar for that. The Pop It didn't happen on a big pitch, the way stories sometimes told it. There was no dramatic snap heard across a stadium. No slow-motion collapse.

It happened on a boring throw in a Saturday morning pool game at a tournament complex that looked like every other tournament complex.

Top of the third. Runner on first. One out. The opposing coach put on a steal.

"Up!" Kyle called, sliding his feet, ready to throw through. The pitch came in high. He came out of his crouch clean, transfer smooth, arm slot where it was supposed to be.

As he started forward, he felt it—a sharp, hot tug along the inside of his elbow, like someone had reached in and plucked one string too hard.

The ball left his hand late. It sailed over second, tailing right. Tyler, at short, leapt, got fingertips on it, and knocked it down enough to keep it in the infield.

The runner was safe by three steps. "Come on, Ky," someone shouted from the dugout. "You had him." Kyle flexed his hand once, twice, trying to shake the feeling out. He could still close his fist, but something in the hinge felt wrong, like the door had shifted on its frame.

He crouched back down. You stayed in. Between innings, Tyler jogged in and flipped him the ball. "You good?" he asked.

"Yeah," Kyle lied. "Just slipped." He threw back to the pitcher. The ball made it there. The pain did too. By the fifth, every throw back to the mound felt like someone was jabbing a thumb into the same small point. He started short-arming the ball, trying to protect the joint. His throws to second lost their carry; Coach Rick called for more pitchouts instead of straight-throughs.

After the game, as the boys dragged their bags toward the lot, Tyler fell in step beside him.

"You're not okay," he said quietly. Kyle's right arm hung a little stiff at his side. "I'm fine," he said. "We've got another game in two hours. I'll be fine by then."

Tyler stopped walking. "No," he said. "You won't." Kyle kept going.

"If I say something, they'll sit me," he said. "Then Moose has to catch, and he hates it, and we look sloppy, and—" "And you're telling me you'd rather wreck your arm than disappoint Coach Rick for one afternoon?"

Tyler snapped. Kyle's eyes flashed.

"I'd rather not be the reason you don't get seen," he said, too loud. The words hung there.

Tyler shut his mouth. They walked the rest of the way in silence. Sideline Diagnosis The next game, Kyle caught the first inning and a half. He blocked balls like nothing was wrong. His glove work was crisp. His footwork on throws was still there; the ball just didn't listen.

A throw back to the mound cut the corner of the plate. Another kicked dirt off the white. Rick's eyes narrowed behind his sunglasses.

"You tired?" he asked between innings. "Little," Kyle said. "I'm good." Third inning. Another steal. Another pop from his elbow. This one louder in his own head.

He came up out of his crouch and the ball slipped, sailing so far up the line that no one even bothered to pretend they had a play.

This time he couldn't hide the wince. His hand went to his arm before he could think about it.

Rick called time and jogged out. "What's wrong?" he asked, low enough that the stands wouldn't hear. "Nothing," Kyle said, teeth clenched.

"Don't lie to me," Rick said. "You're not hitting the pitcher in warmups. Your release point's all over. Did you bang it?"

Kyle swallowed. "It... feels weird," he admitted. "Like... hot. I don't know."

Rick watched him for a beat. "You can squeeze my hand?" he asked. Kyle did. Grip was fine.

"Straighten it all the way." He tried. The joint balked halfway, like someone had slipped sand into it. Rick exhaled through his nose.

"Alright," he said. "You're done for the day. Moose, gear up. Ky, grab some ice." "I can stay in," Kyle protested. "Really. It's—" "You're done," Rick said, voice going coach-flat. "I'm not getting sued because you're stubborn."

The word sued made a few heads turn. Tommy, who had been watching from the baseline, was already moving. Kyle walked off the field feeling smaller than he had in a long time.

Parents offered half-smiles as he passed, sympathy tinged with something else—relief it wasn't their kid.

On the bench, he wrapped an ice pack around his elbow with his left hand, jaw clenched so tight it made his temples throb.

Tommy knelt in front of him. "Can you move your fingers?" he asked. Kyle flexed them. They worked.

"Can you straighten it?" Tommy asked.

Kyle tried. The joint refused. "It's fine," he said. "It's not broken. It'll loosen up." "Fine doesn't look like that," Tommy said softly. "You can't even bend to pick up the Gatorade."

He looked at Rick. "You pulling him for the weekend?" he asked. Rick hesitated, already glancing at the schedule for tomorrow's bracket play.

"Let's see how it feels in the morning," he said. "Could just be a stinger. Kids bounce back quick."

Karyn, who had driven separately and arrived late from a shift, heard that last sentence as she came down the bleachers.

"No," she said, flat as a slammed door. "He's done. For more than tomorrow, probably."

Rick turned, hands up. "Karyn, I get it," he said. "You're a nurse. You see worst-case scenarios. But I see athletes. Some soreness is part of the grind."

She stepped between him and her son. "I see overuse," she said. "I see a fourteen-year-old who's caught more innings this month than most college kids do in a season. This isn't grind. This is neglect."

The word hung there, heavier than sued. Rick's jaw tightened.

"We monitor pitch counts," he said. "We're careful. We —" "You monitor the guys on the mound," she interrupted. "You don't chart the ones in gear who squat through every pitch and throw every ball back. You don't track how many pens he's caught on top of games. We do. Now we're done."

She turned to Kyle, her voice softening. "We're going to see a doctor," she said. "Today if we can." Kyle nodded, throat thick.

"I'm sorry," he said. "For what?" she asked. "For... messing up," he said. "For not being tougher."

Her eyes went bright. "You didn't mess up," she said. "Your body told the truth after your mouth spent months trying not to."

Waiting Room Urgent care on a Saturday afternoon smelled like chlorine wipes and old magazines.

Kyle sat in a chair that was a little too small, arm in a makeshift sling made from one of Tommy's old T-shirts. Tyler sat beside him, fidgeting with a paper clip he'd found on the reception desk.

Karyn paced near the door. Tommy filled out forms. How did the injury occur? He stared at the blank line for a long moment, then wrote: Repeated stress from catching and throwing. No single incident. The line looked too small to hold the truth.

A nurse called Kyle's name. They took his vitals, then led him to an exam room where everything was a shade of tired blue. A doctor in his fifties came in, sleeves rolled up, a wedding ring shining when he washed his hands.

"So," he said, sitting on the rolling stool, "tell me what happened." Kyle shrugged with his good shoulder.

"I caught a lot," he said. "Then it started to hurt. Then it kinda popped." The doctor nodded like he'd heard that story a hundred times, which he probably had. "Where does it hurt?" he asked. Kyle pointed.

"In here," he said. "On the inside. And when I try to straighten it, it feels... stuck."

The doctor palpated along the joint, pressing fingers into tendons and bone. Kyle flinched once, twice. The doctor's mouth flattened.

"Any numbness?" he asked. "Tingling in your fingers?" "A little," Kyle said. "Sometimes."

He tested range of motion. Flexion. Extension. Pronation. Supination. The elbow protested with each.

"Okay," the doctor said finally. "The good news is, it's not dislocated. And if it were fully torn, you'd know. You'd be in a whole lot more distress."

"So he's fine," Tyler blurted, too quickly. The doctor shook his head.

"No," he said. "He's injured. It's just not an ambulance injury. It's a calendar and choices injury."

He looked at Karyn and Tommy. "We're going to get X-rays," he said. "Maybe an MRI later if we need it. My guess is we're dealing with a growth plate issue or a partial strain of the ulnar collateral ligament. Either way, he needs rest. Real rest. Weeks, not days."

"Can he still hit?" Kyle asked. "Can he still breathe?" the doctor shot back. "Yes. That doesn't mean he should go run a marathon with pneumonia."

He softened the tone a bit. "Look," he said. "I know the culture. I've got kids in this world too. There's pressure to play through pain. To make every tryout. To never say no. But here's the thing: your ligaments don't care about anyone's schedule. They don't know what a showcase is. They just know how many times they've been asked to hold when you throw."

He turned the stool to face the parents fully. "When I was a resident," he said, "we saw these injuries in nineteen, twenty-year-olds. Maybe a college pitcher here and there. Now? I see twelve and thirteen-year-olds with more mileage on their elbows than some pros. That's not normal. That's broken."

Karyn's eyes glistened. She nodded slowly. "What do we do?" she asked. "Shut him down," the doctor said. "From catching, from pitching, from throwing competitively. Let the inflammation calm. Get him into physical therapy. If the MRI shows more, we'll talk. But right now, the most important word in his vocabulary is 'no.'" He looked at Kyle. "You know how to say that?" he asked.

Kyle swallowed. "I've never been very good at it," he admitted. The doctor smiled, just a little.

"Your arm's trying to say it for you," he said. "Maybe listen." The Call On the drive home, the car was quieter than usual.

Kyle stared out the window with his left hand, of all things, draped around his neck. His right arm, cradled in the sling, seemed to exist in some other dimension.

Tyler picked at a loose thread on his jeans. "I'm sorry," he said finally.

"For what?" Kyle asked, not looking at him. "For... needing you back there so much," Tyler said. "For not noticing sooner." "You tried," Kyle said. "You told me to sit. I didn't listen." Silence.

From the front seat, Tommy exhaled. "We all missed it," he said. "We saw the ice and the Advil and told ourselves it was normal."

He signaled, pulled into a turnout by a small park, and put the car in park. "What are you doing?" Tyler asked.

"I'm calling Rick," Tommy said. "Now. Before we talk ourselves into half-measures." He stepped out of the car, pacing a small circle on the gravel shoulder as the phone rang. "Tommy," Rick answered, bright as always. "How's our guy?"

"Injured," Tommy said. "Doctor says growth plate stress or partial UCL strain. He's shut down. No catching, no throwing, no tournaments, no pens. For weeks at minimum."

There was a pause.

"Tommy," Rick said, "I'm sorry to hear that. Really. But maybe we can talk about modifying his workload instead of full shutdown. Let him DH, maybe catch a few bullpens. We've got some big events coming. This is a huge summer for his development."

Tommy stared at the hood of the car. "He's fourteen," he said. "He's already caught more innings than most kids his age. We're not bargaining with his elbow so we can make a bracket in June."

"You don't want him to fall behind," Rick said. "Other kids are grinding."

"He's been grinding," Tommy replied. "That's why we're here. We'll keep you posted. But for now, plan like Kyle's not available. He isn't."

He hung up before the conversation could bend back into sales. When he got back in the car, Karyn took his hand and didn't say anything. They drove home. Benched Being told to rest sounded great in theory. In practice, it erased him from the thing he loved.

At school, Kyle's teammates asked how long he'd be out. "Couple weeks, maybe," he said at first.

After the MRI, the estimate stretched. "Doctor says six to eight," he said. "Maybe more if PT is slow." Some kids nodded sympathetically. Others just shrugged and started talking about who would catch now.

At the Academy, it was worse.

For the first time in years, Kyle sat in the bleachers while other kids caught his brother's bullpens. He watched them jab their mitts at borderline pitches, heard them drop blocks he would've smothered, saw Tyler shake them off on signs they called half-heartedly.

Every mistake itched under his skin. "You can come down and shadow them if you want," Rick said once. "Help coach 'em up. Stay engaged."

Kyle shook his head. "If I'm down there, I'll try to throw," he said. "Doctor said no." Rick's jaw tightened just a hair.

"Gotta be careful with doctors," he said. "Sometimes they wrap kids in bubble wrap. Baseball's not a bubble-wrap sport."

Karyn, who had insisted on being there that night, stepped forward. "Baseball also isn't supposed to be a surgery-at-sixteen sport," she said. "He'll be at Veterans with Jack some days. He can work on footwork and receiving with no throws. He'll be fine."

Rick held up his hands. "Hey, I'm just saying what I see," he said. "Lots of kids play year-round. They're fine." "Lots of kids aren't," Karyn replied. "We're trying to keep ours in the right column."

* * *

The first night Kyle slept with the sling, he couldn't sleep. He lay on his back because that was the only way the elbow didn't bark, and he stared at the ceiling and listened to Tyler's even breathing across the room and tried not to think about anything.

He thought about everything.

He thought about the first time he'd put on the gear, in fourth grade, when Coach Penney had said catcher's the only position with a tool you can't do without and he'd liked the word tool, the seriousness of it. He thought about the way other kids' fathers had looked at him after a long inning, with a kind of approval he had not had to earn from his own father, who approved of him without conditions and so didn't notice when Kyle stayed in too long. He thought about how he had said I'm fine at every fork in this road. He thought, for the first time clearly, that maybe he had not become a catcher because he loved being a catcher. Maybe he had become a catcher because he had been good at not saying when something hurt.

He turned his head to the wall. The wall did not have an opinion. He was grateful for the wall.

After a long time he rolled over very carefully and got the elbow into the position the doctor had shown them, and after a longer time, he slept.

***

Jack's Bench

Cedarbrook Field felt different with a sling. Kyle sat on the top row of the bleachers, right arm hugged close, left hand drumming on his knee. Below, Jack ran a small-group practice. Ground balls. Fly balls. Rundowns. The usual.

After a while, Jack climbed the steps and dropped down beside him, knees cracking.

"How's the equipment?" he asked, nodding at the elbow. "Annoyed," Kyle said. "Doctor says it wants a vacation." "Doctor's got good instincts," Jack said.

They watched in silence for a minute. "I feel useless up here," Kyle confessed. "You're not," Jack said. "You're getting a view most catchers never see. They're always in the middle. They don't realize what the whole thing looks like."

Kyle squinted at the field. "You mean like... positioning?" he asked.

"Positioning," Jack said. "Body language. Tempo. Who backs up, who drifts. You can learn a lot about a team from the way they treat dead time."

Down below, a kid booted a routine grounder. His shoulders slumped. The shortstop glared. No one said a word.

"Noted," Jack said under his breath. "That's the kind of thing a college coach notices from a lawn chair. Doesn't make any list, but it matters."

"That's what you write in your book?" Kyle asked. Jack patted his back pocket.

"I don't carry it on paper anymore," he said. "But yeah. Stuff like that." Kyle watched another rep. This time, when someone missed, Tyler jogged over, said something quick, and slapped the kid's shoulder. The difference in the next play was obvious.

Jack smiled. "How's it feel," he asked, "knowing this wouldn't be happening if you were back there doing everything for them?"

Kyle shrugged, then winced. "I don't know," he said. "Weird. Good weird. Bad weird. Both." Jack nodded.

"That's honest," he said. "Injuries stink. Rest feels like punishment when you're wired to work. But sometimes the only way a team learns how to share the load is if the kid who always carries it has to sit."

He paused. "And sometimes the only way a kid learns to say 'enough' is when his body does it for him."

Kyle picked at a splinter in the bleacher. "I hate that it had to be this way," he said.

"So do I," Jack said. He didn't say more for a while. He just watched the field.

Down below, Tyler waved a fielder a step to his left. The next ball found him exactly where he'd been moved.

"Catchers aren't equipment," Jack said finally, almost to himself. "They're kids with elbows that don't come with replacement parts. People keep forgetting that one."

Kyle snorted softly. "Feels like I could use one."

"Not yet. You caught this in time."

He stood. "Come on. I need you to help me see something. Coach's eyes miss stuff sometimes. You can be my scout. That arm might be on the shelf, but your brain's still under warranty."

He said it lightly, but Kyle heard the respect under the joke. He followed Jack down the steps, sling and all.

For the rest of the practice, he stood near home plate, calling out where runners should have gone, who should have backed up which base. At first, his voice came uncertain, barely above the wind. By the end, he was louder.

Kids listened.

Rankings and Red Ink

A week after the diagnosis, ProspectMap updated its lists. Tyler's name stayed where it was. Kyle's, which had never appeared, still didn't. But tucked under the positional rankings was a new column: Injury Notes: A few names had little red crosses beside them with short blurbs. Out with shoulder strain. Elbow soreness, expected back mid-July. Season-ending surgery.

Marco texted Tyler a screenshot. Yo. They're listing injuries now. This is creepy. Tyler stared at the screen, then before he could overthink it, he turned his phone toward Kyle.

"Look," he said. "They're tracking who's hurt now." Kyle read it once, jaw tightening.

"I'm glad I'm invisible," he said. He handed the phone back and walked away. Later, at the kitchen table, Tommy opened his notebook again. Under "Non-money cost," he added a new line.

One right elbow, overdrawn. He stared at the line until it went soft at the edges, then closed the cover and reached for Mary's ledger on the shelf above the coffee tin.

He ran his hand over the worn leather. The pages inside had once tracked bread and rent and baseballs for Cedarbrook Field. Numbers that meant survival, not status.

He opened to a blank page and wrote a new heading in careful block letters.

What we will not spend.

He didn't fill it in yet. But the first entry was already forming, somewhere between his chest and the sound of his younger son's laugh when he forgot about the sling for a minute and joined a dumb joke at dinner.

Kyle's arm would heal, eventually. The MRI would show strain, not rupture. The therapy bands would hang from doorknobs. The rubber ball for grip strength would live on the coffee table. The calendar would tilt around PT appointments instead of tournaments for a while.

But something deeper had torn that spring, too. The idea that a kid could absorb anything you asked him to absorb. That, finally, had given way.

ORTHOPEDIST'S OFFICE—CLIPBOARD LIGHT

The waiting room smelled like antiseptic and old magazines. Posters of joints lined the walls, bright diagrams of human hinges.

Kyle sat with his arm in a sling, trying to look tougher than he felt. Tyler sat beside him, quiet, eyes fixed on the floor like he could hold it in place.

The doctor was kind and blunt. "He needs rest," she said. "No throwing for four weeks. Then physical therapy."

Karyn exhaled. Rest sounded like relief. Then Tommy's phone buzzed with a text from Coach Carver, the man who never watched a full inning but always knew where the money went.

CARVER: Heard about Kyle. We need clearance through our program. Liability. Also—showcase is in three weeks. Spots will be reassigned if athletes aren't available.

Tommy stared at the screen. The words liability and spots sat next to each other, clinical and cold.

"They can't," Karyn whispered after he showed her. "They can't punish a kid for being hurt."

Tommy thought, briefly, of Jack's stories about the field — the way paper could turn play into trespass. Different era, same trick.

He typed back: Doctor says rest. We're resting. The reply came fast.

CARVER: Understood. Just confirming you're withdrawing from the showcase. We'll proceed accordingly.

Proceed accordingly. Like a court order. Kyle looked up. "Am I... in trouble?" he asked, voice small. "No," Tommy said too quickly. "You're hurt. That's not trouble."

But Tyler's eyes flicked to the phone and stayed there. He'd already learned the equation: availability equals worth.

In the car afterward, no one turned on the radio. The silence had a shape — the four of them sitting inside a system that pretended it was about baseball.

At a stoplight, Tyler spoke without looking at anyone. "If I get hurt," he said, "we don't tell them."

Karyn's head snapped around. "Don't you say that," she said, voice sharp with fear.

Tyler shrugged, defensive. "That's what they do." Tommy gripped the steering wheel until his knuckles went white. He wanted to pull the car over, to pull his boys out of all of this, to drive them to a field where no one had a clipboard.

Instead, he drove home, and the cost settled into the seats with them.

Chapter Nine — The Line in the Ledger

THE LEDGER CAME DOWN from the shelf the same way the good dishes did. Carefully. With both hands. On a night that felt bigger than it looked.

Tuesday started like any other and kept taking weight. By supper the rain still hadn't shown, the air felt swollen, and the Ruggiero kitchen hummed under the overhead light. Mail sat in a crooked stack beside the salt shaker. In the middle of the table lay the only thing that did not belong to the day: Mary Davis's ledger.

The cover was worn to soft brown, edges darkened where thumb and finger had met it for years. The elastic that had once held it shut had long since surrendered; a rubber band now did the work. The corners of a few old receipts peeked out like bookmarks from another decade.

Tommy took a breath he hadn't realized he was holding and slid the rubber band off. "You sure about this?" he asked.

Karyn, arms folded across her chest, nodded toward the book. "You're the one who pulled it down off the shelf," she said. "If we're going to keep pretending we're making grown-up decisions, we might as well use grown-up tools."

Mary had been gone only since the spring — a quiet stroke in her sleep after Tommy and Karyn had moved into the house on Chestnut Street. Jack had found the ledger on her kitchen table the morning after, still opened to the page she had last worked on that winter — a Christmas card to Ann Belmonte, the thirtieth in the column, the entry not yet finished. He had closed the book gently and brought it home with him and put it on a high shelf above the coffee tin, where he could see it from the chair he sat in to put on his boots.

He had brought it down for the Ruggieros a month ago. Not a gift. A loan, the way you loan somebody a tool when you can see they've started the kind of job they aren't going to finish without it. Tommy had asked him once if he was sure. Jack had said the only way Mary's book did any good was open on a kitchen table with people arguing over it, and that hadn't been his kitchen table for a long time.

Jack sat at the far side of the table, chair tipped back just enough to make Karyn nervous, elbows resting on his knees. For once, he was in a collared shirt instead of his usual windbreaker, though the shirt was as old as the fence.

"I'll try not to spill coffee on church history," he said. He reached over and rested two fingers on the cover.

"Mary used to say this thing weighed more than the nails," he said. "The wood was Fred and George's job. The numbers were hers."

Tommy opened to the first page. The early entries were neat, narrow, and practical. May 1970 – Fence boards, 72 at.89 – $64.08 May 1970 – Nails, 10 lbs – $7.50 June 1970 – Chalk, 3 bags – $4.20 June 1970 – Hot dogs, buns, onions (opening day) – $32.17 Every few lines, in smaller handwriting, Mary had added notes that weren't about dollars at all.

Tommy Howard's grandmother insisted on paying double for lemonade. Refunded half in hot dogs. Fred says fence will last 10 years. George says kids will. We'll see who's right.

As the years went on, the entries shifted. Field maintenance. Fundraising. Hospital bills. Quiet donations from people who signed their names smaller than the numbers.

The town's whole heart, written in ink. Tommy flipped ahead carefully, past the pages that belonged to other battles —Hartwell meetings, legal fees, years when the field had come close to being swallowed whole—and stopped at one of the few blank spreads left.

Earlier that week, after Kyle's MRI and a long night of not sleeping, he'd opened the ledger and written a single line at the top of that page.

WHAT WE WILL NOT SPEND. Now, under the same heading, the ink looked almost too thin for what they were about to put on it.

The Kids in the Other Room

In the living room, the television murmured. Tyler and Kyle sat shoulder to shoulder on the couch, a bowl of popcorn between them. The sling was gone now, replaced by a simple brace and a list of exercises taped to the fridge.

Tyler held the remote loosely, thumb hovering but still. His eyes weren't really on the screen. "You think they're talking about me?" he asked, quietly.

"I think they're talking about us," Kyle said. "And about this." He lifted his right arm a few inches.

It moved, but carefully, like it was on a new hinge. Tyler chewed on that. "I don't like that we made them have a meeting," he said.

"We didn't," Kyle replied. "The machine did. We just brought home the receipts."

On the other side of the wall, a chair scraped and the ledger's pages whispered as they turned.

Columns

"Alright," Karyn said, pulling a ballpoint pen from behind her ear. "If we're going to use this thing, we should do it right."

She drew a line down the center of the blank page, dividing it into two columns. On the left, she wrote: WHAT WE'LL PAY On the right, under Tommy's heading:

WHAT WE WON'T.

The pen dug a little deeper into the paper on that last word. Jack watched, quiet, hands folded.

"Mary would've liked this," he said. "She always said the trick to running a field was knowing which debts were worth collecting and which weren't."

Tommy nodded. "The trick to running a family might be the same," he said. He sat back, looking at the columns.

"Okay," he said. "What goes where?" Karyn didn't hesitate. "Gas," she said. "Hotel rooms once in a while. Good cleats. Decent food on the road so they don't live on nachos and Slurpees. That can go in what we'll pay."

She wrote: Gas, hotels sometimes, real meals. Tommy added: Tournaments that make sense. Camps with people we trust. He paused, then added in smaller letters: Not every one they advertise. He shifted the pen to the right-hand column. "What we won't," he said, "is easier."

He wrote: Elbows. Backs. Sleep. Schoolwork. Whole seasons at a time. Karyn leaned in. "Joy," she said. "We're not spending their joy." She'd already written it once in her own notebook after that first tournament weekend—Joy:?— and the question mark had been haunting her ever since.

This time she left no space for punctuation. Joy. Jack cleared his throat.

"And you're not spending the field," he said. They looked at him.

"What do you mean?" Tommy asked. Jack gestured out the window, toward the darkness where Veterans sat.

"You start trading too many nights there for fluorescent lights in a warehouse," he said, "and this place becomes a story instead of a place. The creek doesn't know what a prospect ranking is. It just knows whether kids are there throwing rocks in it."

Karyn nodded slowly. "So we write it down," she said. She added to the WHAT WE WON'T SPEND side: Cedarbrook Field. Tommy smiled despite himself. "You know how crazy that would sound in one of those parent meetings?" he said. "'We've decided not to spend our neighborhood field.'" "Good thing we're not voting on it there," Jack said.

The Cost So Far

They sat back for a moment, looking at the headings, the first few entries. "Feels like we should put an honest number on what we already spent," Tommy said. "Just to see it." He reached into the pile of crumpled receipts and printed emails he'd brought home from the glove compartment and the kitchen drawer and spread them across the table. Tournament fees. Parking.

Hotel folios. Camp registrations. "Optional" gear packages. Karyn pulled out her own folded paper—the one she'd started at 4:27 a.m. before that first tournament and kept adding to in the months since.

"First tournament," she read. "Three games, two nights, four hundred and thirty-seven dollars. Plus sore arm, sore knees, joy with a question mark." She laid it flat in the center, like an exhibit.

Tommy added up the dollar amounts from memory. "If I had to guess," he said, tapping the paper, "we're north of three grand this year on just the machine stuff. Not counting town ball. Not counting school."

He shook his head. "I worked a lot of Saturdays to make that money," he said. "And I'd do it again if I knew every dime bought them something they actually needed."

Karyn pointed to Kyle's exercise sheets on the fridge. "We bought an injury," she said. "And a lot of car time. And a few good weekends, sure. But we also bought pressure they didn't ask for at thirteen."

She reached for the ledger and wrote on the right-hand side: One elbow (overdrawn). Tommy watched the words soak into the page. It was confession more than accounting.

"We're not the only ones," he said. "Every tournament we go to, there's some kid with ice on his shoulder in between games. Some parent saying, 'He'll be fine by next weekend.' "

Jack nodded slowly. "In the seventies, when George started bringing me around here," he said, "we had kids with aches. Sore backs. Bruised ankles. Torn-up hands from shoveling. We didn't see elbows like this. Not on boys who still needed rides to school."

He looked up. He didn't say more for a beat. Then he tapped the ledger.

"This is the right book to be writing in," he said.

The Kids' Column "Do they get a say?" Karyn asked.

"In what we won't spend?" Tommy said. "In any of it," she said. "I don't want to swing too far the other way and make decisions over their heads because we're spooked."

She wasn't a fan of pendulums. They tended to knock things over on both swings.

Jack smiled. "Ask them," he said. "But ask better questions than, 'Do you want to quit?' " He leaned forward.

"Ask what they'd miss," he said. "Ask what they'd keep if they could only pick a few things. Sometimes kids know more about enough than we do."

They called the boys in. Tyler paused the movie without complaint. Kyle stood up a little slower, bracing his right arm with his left out of habit.

When they walked into the kitchen and saw the ledger on the table, both stopped.

"Are we in trouble?" Tyler asked, only half-joking. "Not yet," Tommy said. "We're having a meeting. You're part of it." He gestured to the chairs. "Sit," he said. "Please." They did.

Karyn turned the ledger so they could see the headings. "What we'll pay," she read, pointing. "What we won't." Tyler frowned. Kyle tilted his head. "Is this about money?" Tyler asked.

"It's about cost," Tommy said. "Money's part of that. So's time. So's stuff you can't put a dollar sign next to."

"We're not quitting baseball," Tyler said quickly. "No one said that," Karyn replied. "We're asking what it should look like. For real. Not just because some calendar or coach says so."

She slid the pen across the table. "If you could pick three things that you love most about this game," she said, "just three you'd keep no matter what—what would they be?" Tyler looked at the page, at the slowly filling columns, at the worn cover. "Playing shortstop," he said. "Like, really playing it. Reading hops. Making plays. That feeling when you throw a guy out by half a step and the dugout loses its mind."

Karyn wrote under the left column: Real reps at short.

"Okay," she said. "What else?" Tyler thought.

"Pitching when I'm fresh," he said. "Not when my arm feels like someone swapped it out for a dead fish."

They both glanced at Kyle's elbow. Karyn added: Pitching rested, not just available. Kyle cleared his throat. "Catching when I can actually feel my hand," he said. "Working with pitchers. Getting better at that... quiet stuff. Framing. Calling the right pitch. Making guys look good."

He paused. "And Veterans," he added. "Wednesdays. Summers. Just... being there." Tommy smiled.

"You're stealing our material," he said. "We already wrote that one." They all looked at the WHAT WE WON'T SPEND side, at the word Cedarbrook Field.

Tyler studied the page. "Can I add something there?" he asked, pointing to the right column. Karyn slid the ledger and pen toward him. He hesitated, then wrote carefully: Playing hurt so someone else doesn't have to be uncomfortable.

The room went quiet. "Where'd that come from?" Tommy asked, gently. Tyler glanced at Kyle.

"I made you catch a lot of pens you shouldn't have," he said. "Because it was easier than telling Coach I didn't want some other kid back there. That's on me."

Kyle shook his head.

"I said yes," he replied. "That's on me." Jack cleared his throat.

"Funny thing about big machines," he said. "They only work if everybody agrees to pretend they're the only way. Somebody starts saying no, the gears start to slip."

He tapped Tyler's line. "That's a good 'no' to write down," he said. Karyn added, just below it: Saying yes out of fear. Then, in smaller handwriting: Fear-based decisions. Machine wins every time with those. Tyler leaned back. "So... what does this actually change?" he asked. "Are we dropping the team? Are we not going to tournaments? Are we just playing at Veterans now?"

He sounded less defiant than scared. Tommy rubbed his jaw. "I don't think it's all or nothing," he said. "You love your Elite team. There are good coaches there. You've learned things. We're not going to pretend that doesn't exist."

He looked at Jack. "But we're not letting it be the only voice anymore," he added. Jack nodded.

"But we're not letting it be the only voice anymore," Tommy added. "Fewer tournaments. More built-in rest. Non-negotiable time at the field down the street. And if a coach's plan doesn't fit that, we look at each other before we look at them."

Tyler swallowed. "And if they say I'll fall behind?" he asked.

"Then we remember that falling behind what isn't the same as falling behind who you're supposed to be," Tommy said.

Jack, who had not said much for a while, pushed back from the table.

"I've sat on a lot of lawn chairs," he said. "I've watched a lot of clipboard guys. The ones worth playing for don't need your whole childhood on tape. They need a few good looks at a kid who knows who he is and still loves the game at seventeen."

He stood, looked at the ledger, didn't add anything to it.

"That's your page," he said. "Mine's out at the field."

Karyn capped the pen, then uncapped it again. There was one more thing she needed to write. Under WHAT WE WON'T SPEND, she added: Family dinners more than three nights a week.

Tyler blinked. "We're... we're not allowed to miss dinner?" he asked.

"You're allowed to miss plenty of things," she said. "Homework. A joke. A bus. Dinner is where I see your faces. I'm not trading that away three seasons in a row so you can sit in another hotel room eating cold pizza between pool games."

She underlined it once.

"Family dinner," she said. "That's our showcase." Tommy laughed, but his eyes were bright.

"What about cost?" he asked. "Real cost. We still need to think about that."

He pointed to the left-hand column. "We can't swipe a card at every 'optional' thing," he said. "Optional might as well mean mandatory the way they say it, but it's not. Every time we sign up for something, it has to clear this page."

Tyler nodded slowly.

"So if Coach emails another skills camp," he said, "we ask: Does it help my arm? My joy? My field? Or is it just another notch in their ledger?"

"Exactly," Karyn said.

As they sat there, phones facedown for once, one of them buzzed against the wood. Karyn flipped it over. A new email from the Academy: Don't let your player fall behind this summer! Spots still available in our Elite Exposure Series. Four weekends, twelve games, full metrics package, college coaches on site. Payment plans available. This is where the serious families separate themselves.

She read it once, then looked at the ledger. Without saying a word, she slid the phone across the table. Tommy read it, then Jack.

Tyler watched their faces. "What do we do?" he asked. Tommy picked up the pen.

In the margin beside WHAT WE WON'T SPEND, he wrote: Four consecutive weekends at the mercy of a subject line.

Then he clicked the email open again, scrolled to the bottom, and hit delete.

"Feels like vandalism," he said. "In a good way." Karyn exhaled, tension she'd been carrying between her shoulder blades easing half an inch. "Okay," she said. "Then it's decided." She drew a box around the page, like a frame.

"This isn't about being anti-academy," she added. "It's about being pro-us. Pro-kids. Pro-field. Next time someone tries to tell us what serious families do, we can say, 'We're serious enough to know our limits.' " Ledger Entry Later that night, after the boys had gone back to their movie and Jack had left with a promise to "hold your spot on Wednesdays," Tommy sat alone at the table with the ledger in front of him.

The house had gone mostly quiet. The fridge hummed. Rain ticked lightly against the window over the sink.

He flipped back a few pages, past the old entries about boards and chalk and Hartwell votes and hospital bills. Past the line Mary had written in 1978— Some costs don't show up until years later. Pay attention. He thought about his father, who had never seen radar guns at youth games but had known something about invisible expenses anyway. He thought about George and Mary, about the night a gunshot in a restaurant parking lot had started all of this.

What would they think of ranking sites and four-figure summers and kids with ice packs at fourteen?

He didn't know. But he knew what they'd say about a family that sat down with a ledger and tried to draw lines around what mattered.

He picked up the pen one more time and, under everything else, wrote: Tonight – decided that "enough" is not failure. It's a fence you build on purpose.

He closed the ledger gently, the way he'd watched Jack close the gate at Veterans a thousand times.

Tomorrow, there would still be emails and tournaments and rankings and conversations in bleachers. The machine wouldn't shut itself off.

But Cedarbrook Field would still be there. And now, in ink thick enough to feel, there was a record that the Ruggieros had chosen a side. Not against baseball.

For it.

Chapter Ten — The College Talk

Mid-2000s · Between Cedarbrook Field and Everywhere Else

THE FIRST TIME SOMEONE called him "Tyler's brother," Kyle pretended not to hear it.

They were at a spring showcase in a town that smelled like mulch and chain restaurants. Tyler had just finished a round of batting practice in front of a half-circle of clipboards. The numbers on the screen behind the cage had flashed big enough for parents to read from the aluminum stands.

"Eighty-one off the bat," the operator said, pleasantly surprised. "Nice jump, kid."

A coach in a college pullover nodded, made a note, and asked Tyler his last name again.

"Ruggiero," Tyler said, breathless in that good way. "Tyler Ruggiero." The coach squinted at the sheet.

"Ruggiero... Ruggiero..." he murmured. "You related to the other Ruggiero that was here a couple years ago? The pitcher?"

Tyler glanced past the cage, toward the bullpen where Kyle stood with a bag of balls and a bucket turned upside down for whoever needed a seat.

"Yeah," he said. "He's my brother." "Oh," the coach replied, already moving on. "So you're Kyle's brother." Later, near the snack stand, two dads leaned on the rail, watching Tyler field grounders at third during infield drills. "Who's the kid at third?" one asked.

"Ruggiero," the other said. "Tyler. The younger one. His brother used to be the arm. Now it's his turn."

He jerked his chin toward the bullpen without looking. "You know how it goes," he added. "One brother gets the gas, the other gets the gear bag."

Kyle heard that part. His thumb, still taped under the brace on bad days, tightened around the ball he was holding.

He rolled his shoulder once, let the comment pass through him like cold air, and tossed the next warm-up pitch back to a kid he barely knew.

"Next," he called. "Let's go. Don't let my old bones show you up." The kid laughed and stepped on the mound.

Two Calendars

The fridge had become a scoreboard of its own. On the left side, under a magnet shaped like Fenway, a color-coded calendar laid out Tyler's world.

Monday: Elite practice. Tuesday: School lifting. Wednesday: Veterans, if his arm and homework cooperated. Thursday: "Optional" hitting that wasn't really optional.

Friday–Sunday: some combination of league games, showcase events, and tournaments with names like "Battle at the Border" and "Northeast Exposure Classic."

On the right side, under a Cedarbrook Field bumper sticker Jack had never actually stuck on his truck, a simpler page held Kyle's schedule.

Physical therapy.

Doctor follow-ups.

School games, when the trainer cleared him to catch more than three innings. Wednesdays circled in green: Veterans with Jack.

Saturday mornings: "Little guys" written in Jack's handwriting, meaning the youth clinic Kyle had started helping with.

Most days, the calendars overlapped like competing broadcasts. The family moved through the kitchen reading and re-reading them, trying to make the two shows fit into one television.

One Wednesday in April, Karyn stood between them, coffee in hand. "Tyler's got batting practice at the academy at four," she said.

"Coach says they're bringing in a former pro to work with the infielders on footwork."

She looked to the other side. "Kyle's got PT at three," she went on. "And Jack texted about the Wednesday night game. Said he needs a catcher who can still remember what a kid strike zone looks like."

Tommy leaned against the counter, rubbing his temples. "We can't clone ourselves," he said. "So we pick." Karyn set the mug down.

"We already did," she said. "Last week. And the week before. Ty got the first two. Tonight, I'm taking Kyle to PT, and then to Veterans.

You take Tyler. That way each of them gets one of us." Tommy nodded slowly.

"Split the team," he said. "Run a two-parent defense." He tried to make it sound like a joke. It mostly was not.

Tyler's Track

The academy loved Tyler's numbers. By his sophomore year, he had become one of their favorite talking points. His exit velocity ticked up every testing day. His arm from third base played well on the scoreboard. His 60-yard dash time wasn't elite. But it was solid enough to slot him into the middle of any roster conversation.

"High motor, good arm, projectable frame," Coach Rick told anyone who would listen. "Comes from a baseball family. Brother was a dude on the mound before the injury. Dad's all in. This kid gets it."

At one of the fall "College Night" workouts in the fieldhouse, Tyler stood at the end of the 60-yard line, hands on his knees, heart pounding in that familiar mix of fatigue and hope.

"Seventy-nine across the infield," the metrics guy called after a throw from deep third. "That'll play."

Rick slapped Tyler's back. "Nice," he said. "Keep this up and you're going to have options." Options. Tyler heard the opening in it. He also heard the burden.

In the corner of the warehouse, just beyond the halo of the brightest lights, Kyle sat on a folding chair with a bucket between his feet. A TheraBand dangled from his fingers. He worked his shoulder gently through the exercises the therapist had given him.

Arm out, pull. Arm up, pull. Circles, slow and controlled.

He watched his brother field ground balls and make throws that snapped through the air with a sound Kyle still felt in his own chest.

"You ever miss it?" one of the younger kids asked him between rounds, eyes flicking to Kyle's brace.

"Every day," Kyle said. "You ever wish you could hit like him?" The kid grinned. "Every day," he echoed.

Kyle tossed him a ball. "Then we're even," he said.

When the infield segment ended, Tyler jogged over, hat pushed back, sweat at his temples.

"How's it feel?" Kyle asked, nodding toward his arm. "Good," Tyler said. "They said my hands are 'advanced for my age.' " He did air quotes without meaning to.

"Yeah?" Kyle said. "Did they say your brother's sarcasm is advanced for his age too?"

Tyler laughed. "That's maxed out," he said. "No more room to grow." He took a breath.

"You staying for the recruiting talk?" he asked. "Coach says they'll explain the whole process. Timelines, showcases, all that."

Kyle shook his head. "I've got little guys at Veterans," he said. "Jack's teaching them how to drag the infield without killing themselves. He's making me do the demo."

Tyler rolled his eyes. "Of course he is," he said. "Only you could turn an arm injury into a promotion."

Kyle shrugged. "Somebody's got to yell at them to stop eating the chalk," he said. "Might as well be me."

They bumped fists. "Text me if they tell you anything that doesn't sound like a sales pitch," Kyle said. "If they do, I'll frame it," Tyler replied.

Kyle's Track Cedarbrook Field had no radar gun and no projector screen, but it did have a different kind of list.

On Wednesdays, the group of younger kids who showed up had grown from three to eight to twelve. They came from the neighborhood, from the rec league, from word of mouth. Some wore Elite hats. Some wore hats from teams their parents had found on the internet. Some wore no logo at all.

To Jack, they were just names.

To the kids, Kyle was the guy who could still throw well enough to show them what it was supposed to look like, even if he couldn't do it as long or as hard as he once had.

"Alright," Kyle called one evening, standing at short with a bucket. "We're doing the Big League drill. You mess it up, blame your coach. That's me."

He rolled a ball to a twelve-year-old at third. The kid charged, fielded awkwardly, and double-clutched before throwing.

"Stop," Kyle said, holding up a hand. The boy froze.

"You nervous?" Kyle asked.

"A little," the kid admitted. "That's good," Kyle said. "Means you care. But you know what big leaguers do?" He walked over and pointed at the infield dirt between third and home. "They keep this patch simple. Ball. Hand. Throw.

They let the crowd be loud by itself." He tapped the boy's chest lightly with the back of his glove. "You already know how to do this," he said. "Next rep, pretend it's just you and your dad in the backyard. Or you and your sister. Or you and your dog. Whoever you learned with. Make it that small."

They tried again. Cleaner this time. The throw beat the imaginary runner by half a step.

"There you go," Kyle said. "See? Backyard works." On the fence near right field, Jack watched, arms folded, the faintest of smiles at his mouth.

"You're turning into me," he called when the kids ran to get water. "Is that a compliment or a warning?" Kyle asked.

"Both," Jack said. "You hear yourself out there? Talking more about hearts than hands."

Kyle flushed. "I'm just... trying not to break them before the machine gets a turn," he said.

Jack nodded. "Mary wrote that once," he said. "In the ledger?" Kyle asked.

"In the margin," Jack replied. "When Michael started getting looks, she scribbled, 'Let's make sure the game doesn't break him before life gets its chance.' " He tapped the rail. "Turns out the game and life were the same thing for him," he said, quietly. "I'm still trying to get that right with you lot."

Kyle looked at the kids chasing foul balls down the line, at the sunset bleeding across center.

"You think it's working?" he asked. Jack considered.

"With them?" he said. "Ask me in ten years."

He looked at Kyle. "With you?" he added. "Better than you think."

In the Middle

One night that summer, the brothers sat on opposite ends of the couch, the glow of a laptop between them.

The TV was on mute. The rating site's homepage filled the screen. Tyler scrolled past lists of names arranged by graduation year, position, state. Some had stars beside them. Some had paragraphs. Some had no write-ups at all.

"There," Kyle said, pointing. "That's you." Tyler's name sat in the middle of a long column.

Tyler Ruggiero, INF/RHP, 2020 – High-motor infielder with developing power. Arm plays on the left side. Shows feel on the mound. Needs strength.

Tyler read it twice. " 'Developing power,' " he said. "Feels like they're saying, 'House is okay, still needs a new roof.' " " 'Shows feel on the mound,' " Kyle added. "Means, 'We saw three pitches and he didn't fall down.' " They smiled, but only a little.

"You know what mine said?" Kyle asked. Tyler turned.

"You have a profile?" he said, surprised. "Had," Kyle corrected. "From before. Some camp when I was a freshman. They listed my velo, said I had 'pitcher's build.' That was it."

He shrugged. "I think they took me off the board when I disappeared from the circuit," he said. "Out of sight, out of list."

Tyler felt something twist in his chest. "I'm sorry," he said. "For what?" Kyle asked. "For... still being on here," Tyler said slowly. "For dragging you to half these things when you'd rather be at the field. For being the one with the numbers now."

Kyle stared at him. "Ty," he said. "If you ever apologize again for being good at this, I'm going to make you run poles at Veterans until your legs fall off."

Tyler tried to laugh. "I just don't want you to feel like you got... replaced," he said.

Kyle thought about it for a long second. "I'm doing different things now," he said. "It's not the same thing as nothing." He nudged the laptop closed with his good hand.

Tyler blinked. "You really mean that?" he asked. Kyle thought of the little guys at Veterans, of the way their faces lit up when the ball stuck in their glove for the first time.

"Most days," he said. "On the bad days, when my elbow clicks or some dad says, 'Didn't you used to—' and leaves the sentence open, I miss the other road. But I don't want to trade you spots. Not really."

He nudged Tyler's ankle with his foot. "You understand that, right?" he asked. "We're not auditioning for one role here. This isn't a twobrother show where only one gets to stay. The machine talks like that. The game doesn't."

Tyler swallowed. "I'm trying," he said.

"Good," Kyle replied. "Because I'm planning on free gear when you sign somewhere."

Tyler finally laughed for real. "There it is," he said. "Thought I'd lost your selfish side." The Pull The family still felt the strain, even with the ledger and the rules taped to its inside cover.

One Saturday in July, Tommy sat in the driver's seat of the car, keys in the ignition, torn between two destinations.

Tyler had a doubleheader at the Elite complex, the kind with "coaches in attendance" printed on the flyer. Kyle was helping Jack run a daylong sandlot tournament at Veterans for the neighborhood kids. Three-on-three, make-your-own-rules, winner-stays, loser-picks-the-next-game kind of tournament. The kind you didn't see on any recruiting calendar.

"You can't be two places," Karyn said, standing in the doorway. "We tried that trick already. It ends with you at a rest stop wondering which direction you were supposed to be going."

Tommy rubbed his eyes. "He might get seen today," he said. "Really seen. What if this is one of those days the ledger people talk about? One of those nights we look back on and say, 'That was the moment.' " Karyn stepped closer. "And what if one of those happens at Veterans?" she asked. "What if it's not a scout day but a Jack day? What if the moment isn't a number on a gun but something Kyle says to a kid who needed to hear it?"

He hesitated.

"You're saying I should go to the field," he said. "I'm saying we both know Tyler is going to be surrounded by quarter-zips and clipboards today," she replied. "He will not lack for adult eyes. Kyle will have Jack, sure. But I don't want him to look up at the fence and see an empty spot where his father should be."

Tommy leaned his forehead against the steering wheel. "This felt easier when they were seven," he said.

"No," Karyn said. "It wasn't. We just didn't have as many numbers to hide behind."

She opened the passenger door and slid in.

"I'll go with you to Veterans," she said. "We'll be the loudest cheering section there. Then tonight, when Tyler gets home, we listen to every inning recap like it's the World Series. We tell him we trust him enough to handle one showcase without us breathing down his neck."

Tommy looked at her. "You think that's the right script?" he asked. She shrugged.

"I think it's ours," she said. "That's what the ledger is for. Writing our own."

He turned the key. As they pulled away from the curb, Veterans' light poles were visible at the end of the street.

Under the Lights

That night, Tyler sat on the tailgate of the car with his cleats off, socks gray with infield dust.

"How was it?" Tommy asked, setting a water bottle beside him. "Good," Tyler said. "Okay. I don't know."

He took a long drink. "I played well," he added. "Couple of hits, made some plays. One of the coaches said he liked my hands. Another said I 'run better than the numbers say,' whatever that means."

He shrugged. "Did you miss me?" he asked, half teasing, half serious. Tommy sat on the edge of the bumper.

"Every inning," he said. "And I'm still glad we went where we went." Tyler raised an eyebrow.

"You went to Veterans," he said. It wasn't a question. "We did," Tommy replied.

Tyler chewed the inside of his cheek.

"You pick a good day to skip," he said. "They had a radar gun on every field. You would've loved watching your blood pressure spike."

Tommy smiled. "You mad?" he asked. Tyler thought for a long heartbeat. "A little," he admitted. "But not at you. At how it all makes me feel like I should be mad. Like there's only one way to show you care, and it's to be in the stands every second."

He looked at his father. "You being at Veterans says something too," he said. "Says Kyle's stuff matters even when it doesn't come with stats."

Tommy nodded. "How'd it go there?" Tyler asked. Tommy's face softened. "Kyle was a menace," he said. "In a good way. He and Jack ran this three-on-three game where the kids made their own ground rules. No umpires. Just honor calls. They had to talk close calls out without yelling."

He chuckled. "Mostly worked," he said.

Tommy nudged him with his shoulder. "Point is," he said, "I watched your brother be good at something that doesn't show up on any chart. I don't regret that. And I don't love you one ounce less for not being in the bleachers today. You believe that?"

Tyler looked at the parking lot lights reflecting off the windshield. "I'm working on it," he said. "But yeah. I think I do."

He slid off the tailgate and stood, stretching his back.

"Next week?" he asked. "Next showcase? Will you be there?" Tommy smiled.

"We'll check the ledger," he said. "If the math works, and your arm feels good, and Kyle doesn't need us somewhere else, I'll bring the loudest clap they let in the building."

Tyler grinned. "Deal," he said.

The Long Inning Later that summer, Jack sat on the third-base bleachers at Veterans, watching the brothers take infield together for the first time in months.

Kyle at short, Tyler at third. Ground ball to Tyler. Step, field, fire. Ground ball to Kyle. Glide, field, whip.

The throws met Moose's glove at first with the same sharp sound. "Funny thing," Jack murmured to himself. "The machine only sees one of those arms now."

He thought of Mary's notes in the ledger. Of Michael and Jack. Of how easily one brother's name could swell to fill all the available space if you weren't careful.

Down on the field, a ball took a bad hop and clipped Tyler's shoulder. Kyle laughed and yelled something Jack couldn't hear. Tyler pointed his glove at him, mock offended.

Jack leaned back against the wooden seat. Two boys, the same infield. He let the picture be what it was.

* * *

MOTEL 6 — RUTLAND, VT — 11:47 P.M.

The room had two queen beds, one Tyler and a kid named Brodie from Stoneham, the other Coach Rick on his back with the laptop open on his stomach, blue light on his chin. The air smelled like chlorine from the indoor pool, and the heat was running too high, and Brodie was already snoring. Tyler couldn't sleep.

He had thrown two innings that afternoon at the Northeast Showcase. Six up, six down. Four swinging strikeouts. The radar had liked him. The phone in his pocket had buzzed twice in the dugout afterward with messages from numbers he didn't have saved — one of them somebody from a school in upstate New York whose name he had recognized off a sweatshirt his cousin owned. Coach Rick had clapped his shoulder twice. The clap had been hard the second time, like Rick was making a point with his hand he didn't want to say with his mouth.

Tyler should have felt good. He was sixteen and a college coach had texted him.

He didn't feel good. He felt the way he felt at the end of finals week — a low animal tiredness that didn't belong to a sixteen-year-old, that belonged to the month of Mays and Sundays and gas-station bathrooms his shoulders had been carrying for three years. His elbow had made a small clicking sound on the third pitch of his second inning. He hadn't told anybody. He had thrown the next forty pitches around it.

He slid out of bed in his socks, pulled his hoodie over his T-shirt, and stepped out into the parking lot through the side door that wedged on its hinge. The cold went through his thin sweats right away. He liked it.

Across the lot, an eighteen-wheeler idled, the driver visible inside in profile, eating something out of a paper bag. The pavement was slick with the kind of late-March wet that looked like it hadn't decided whether to be ice. Tyler walked the painted line of a parking space, heel-to-toe, the way Kyle used to make him do when they were six and seven and Kyle had decided a parking space was a balance beam.

He sat down on the curb and put his head in his hands. He had not cried yet today and he was not going to start now. He just wanted to feel his own pulse without thinking about what it was supposed to translate to on someone's spreadsheet.

A long minute went by. Then another.

What he was thinking about, when the cold started getting through, was Cedarbrook. Not the lights. The smell of it. The way the chalk got into your nose if Jack had laid the lines too thick. The sound Marco's glove made — a soft whump, broken-in leather, nothing crisp about it. The way Luis hated to lose three-on-three so much that he would call himself out on a close play just to keep the game from getting tense.

He had not been to a Wednesday night since June.

The truck driver across the lot finished his sandwich, balled up the bag, and pulled away. The diesel sound moved off down the highway and went small. Tyler sat there until his fingers were numb, then went back inside. Coach Rick was asleep with the laptop still open and his glasses on. Tyler closed the laptop carefully, took the glasses off Rick's face, set them on the nightstand, and lay back down on top of his comforter without getting under it. He stayed awake another long time.

He did not call anyone. He did not text Kyle. He did not yet know what he was going to do.

He just knew that the sound he wanted to fall asleep to was Marco's glove.

Chapter Eleven — The Camp

’

Late Summer 2008 · Cedarbrook Field

BY LATE AUGUST, THE season felt like it had been going on for a year and a half.

There had been spring league schedules, summer showcases, “inviteonly” tournaments that turned out to have fifty teams, and one more “can’t-miss” event than anyone could remember. The academy calendar still had fall ball and a winter throwing program circled in confident ink.

Tyler Ruggiero felt all of it in his shoulders every morning when he rolled out of bed.

On a Tuesday afternoon, he stood in front of the fridge, one hand on the freezer handle, the other on the calendar pinned under the Fenway magnet. Next weekend’s box was already filled.

Elite Fall Preview – four games Optional recruiting seminar Metrics re-test – mandatory He stared at it for a long moment, then let the freezer door swing shut. Behind him, Kyle sat at the kitchen table, writing numbers in the margin of Mary’s ledger. He’d borrowed it from Jack the night before “for homework” and never brought it back.

“How bad is it?” Tyler asked, nodding at the page. “Financially?” Kyle said. “On a scale from ‘we should talk’ to ‘sell a kidney,’ we’re somewhere around ‘Mom’s going to keep that pen in her hand until the ink dries out.’ ” He flipped the book so Tyler could see.

On the left side, under WHAT WE’LL PAY, a careful list of camps, tournaments, and gear with check marks beside the ones the family had already agreed to.

On the right side, under WHAT WE WON'T SPEND, a growing column: Four consecutive weekends "just because a subject line tells us to." Playing hurt so someone else doesn't have to be uncomfortable.

Family dinners more than three nights a week. Cedarbrook Field.

Someone—Karyn, by the neatness—had added a new line the night before.

Any more games where you forget you like this. Tyler read it twice. "Little dramatic," he said, but it landed anyway. Kyle watched him.

"You okay?" he asked. Tyler let his forehead rest against the cool metal of the fridge for a second. "I'm tired," he said. "And I feel guilty about being tired. Like I'm not allowed to be if I still want this."

"What's 'this'?" Kyle asked. Tyler waved a hand toward the calendar. "College looks. Numbers that keep going up instead of down. Not being the kid who used to be good."

Kyle flipped the ledger back, closed it gently. "What if we flip the script for one night?" he asked. "Just one." Tyler turned.

"How?" he said. "Cancel a tournament?" "I'm not talking about them," Kyle replied. "I'm talking about us. Jack's been muttering about wanting one game this summer that doesn't belong to any program. No packages. No packages of packages. Just kids and a fence."

"Like the Wednesday nights?" Tyler asked. "Bigger," Kyle said. "Like a... I don't know. A spirit game." He said it lightly. The name stuck anyway.

"You really think kids will show up?" Tyler asked. "You really think they won't?" Kyle shot back. "Half of them complain about the grind every time we're in a hotel lobby. You give them one night with no radar and no clipboards, they'll at least think about it."

Tyler glanced at the calendar again.

"When?" he asked. Kyle checked his watch.

"Tonight," he said. "Before someone fills the box with something else."

Text Invites

Veterans had never needed invitations before. Light and air had always been enough.

But the machine kept kids busy in new ways now. Schedules overlapped. Lives were arranged in spreadsheets and apps.

So Kyle did something that would have made George Davis stare and Mary breathe, "What on earth is a group chat?"

He grabbed his phone and started typing. Veterans tonight. 6:00. No jerseys, no fees, no coaches yelling. Just a game. Bring whoever. If you ask whether it "counts," you're already missing the point. He sent it to everyone he could think of.

Marco. Luis. Moose. A handful of Elite teammates. Two kids from the rec league. One from a rival travel team who always seemed happiest after the last out when the music stopped.

Tyler watched over his shoulder. "You're going to start a turf war," he said. "Field war," Kyle corrected. "Big difference." Replies began to ping back almost immediately.

Dude, seriously? I have lifting at 5. Skip it. Lift dirt. – KB Is this that old field your grandpa built or whatever? Great-grandpa. And yes. – KB Are parents invited? Not as coaches. – KB What team is it for? The one that let you start. – KB Tyler took his phone out and added his own message, sending it to the Elite group.

I'm pitching 6–8 tonight. Veterans. No radar gun. Come if you want to remember why this was fun. He hit send before he could talk himself out of it.

Lighting the Poles

By 5:30, Jack Thompson was in the equipment shed, coaxing the breaker panel the way you coaxed an old car on a cold morning.

The light poles at Veterans didn't like to be rushed. They blinked on in stages, each one humming itself awake, throwing long beams over the grass.

"You sure about this?" he asked as Kyle carried a bucket of balls to home plate. "No," Kyle said. "That's the fun part."

Jack smiled. "Mary always said the best games started with somebody saying 'I'm not sure if we're allowed to do this,' " he said. "You get the word out?"

"Kinda," Kyle replied. "If three kids show up, we'll play three-on--three. If fifteen show up, we'll make up some rules."

Jack nodded toward the ledger, which sat on the dugout bench. "You bring that for luck?" he asked.

"For record-keeping," Kyle said. "In case this turns out to be one of those nights." Jack's eyes softened.

"Most of the nights that matter don't get box scores," he said. "Good instinct bringing a different kind of book."

They walked the field together, checking for rocks in the infield, kicking at a few lumpy patches in shallow left. The fresh chalk glowed in the early evening light.

At ten minutes to six, the driveway was still empty. "You think they all chickened out?" Kyle asked, trying to sound casual. Jack shaded his eyes.

"Give it a minute," he said. "Kids move slow when they're doing something they chose instead of something they were told to do."

As if on cue, the first car turned in. Marco's bike was strapped to the back of it with bungee cords. He hopped off before the tires stopped rolling, helmet already halfway undone. "You're really doing this?" he called. "Depends," Kyle said. "You bring a glove?" Marco held it up.

"Always," he said. Luis arrived next, on his own bike this time, newspaper bag slung over one shoulder. Moose's mom's SUV followed, music leaking out when the doors opened, Moose unfolding himself from the back seat like someone had just let him out of storage.

Then came two more cars, then three. Devon, who played on a rival Elite team but had grown up chasing foul balls at Veterans. Tariq, whose family had never been able to swing academy fees and who had more backyard innings than anyone in town. A quiet kid named Henry who had quit travel ball that spring without telling anybody why.

A minivan pulled up and idled for a second. Tyler stepped out of the passenger side, hat pushed back, glove in hand. Tommy and Karyn climbed out after him, then stopped, taking in the scene.

There was no banner. No registration tent. No laminated rosters. Just a fence, a field, and a growing knot of kids around home plate.

"Looks like your text worked," Tommy said. "Or they're all here for the free concessions," Kyle said. "Which don't exist."

Karyn breathed in, the smell of cut grass and dust filling her lungs. "I like this one better than the complexes," she said. "Parking's terrible, but the view wins."

She and Tommy took seats halfway up the bleachers, next to a small knot of other parents who had apparently gotten the same "not as coaches" memo.

Some still wore Elite gear. Some didn't. Most had brought nothing but water bottles and a willingness, for once, to sit quietly. Draft Day Jack clapped his hands once, loud enough to cut through the chatter. "Alright," he said. "Let's see what we've got here."

Seventeen kids stood on the grass between home and the mound. They ranged from twelve to seventeen. Different teams, different hats, different levels of belief in the whole idea.

"Welcome to the Spirit Game," Jack went on. "Rules are simple." He held up a baseball.

"We're playing until dark," he said. "We're not keeping score on the board. No coach calls, no signs. You call your own fair and foul. Close plays, you work out yourselves. Anybody who starts yelling about a call owes everyone else ice cream later. Questions?"

A hand went up in the back. "Do stats count?" someone asked. Jack thought for a moment.

"In ten years," he said, "you're not going to remember whether you went two for four tonight. You're going to remember who you played with and whether it felt good. So no. Not in the way you mean."

Marco raised his hand. "How do we make teams?" he asked. Jack handed the ball to Kyle.

"Player draft," he said. "Two captains. You and Tyler. Oldest brothers in the room. Makes sense to let you split the town for a night."

Tyler blinked.

"Me?" he said. "Unless you forgot how to read a lineup card," Jack replied. "You boys know each other's games. Figure it out."

They picked teams quickly, like they were seven again. Tyler took Moose at first, Kyle took Marco at short, and the rest sorted itself out — Devon, Tariq, Henry, Luis, two brothers from Maple Street, a lefty ninthgrader Jack liked, mostly. When it was done, they had nine on one side, eight on the other.

"We can play with eight," Kyle said. Jack tossed a spare hat at Tariq.

"You're roving tonight," he said. "You see grass with nobody on it, go stand there."

Game On

They flipped a bat to see who would be home. Tyler's team ended up taking the field first. Kyle's crew batted. No national anthem. No announcements. Just a deep breath, a few claps, and the quiet thud of cleats on dirt.

Tyler walked to the mound, rolling the ball in his hand. Jack met him halfway.

"How's the arm?" Jack asked. "Good," Tyler said. "No games this weekend. No bullpen yesterday. Ledger's clean."

Jack nodded.

"Then here's the deal," he said. "No radar tonight. No pitch count numbers on a board. You go until you feel the kind of tired that means you'll be sore in a way Mary wouldn't approve of. When that happens, you raise your hand like a grown man and say, 'I'm done.' We good?"

Tyler swallowed. "We're good," he said.

"You do that," Jack replied, "and I'll consider this whole experiment a success before we even get through two innings."

He slapped Tyler lightly on the shoulder and walked back to the firstbase line. The first batter was Luis, grinning like someone had handed him a microphone. "Tyler, I'd like a fastball middle-middle, please," he called.

Tyler smirked. "Not on the menu," he said. He delivered an easy firstpitch strike on the outer half. Luis swung out of his shoes and missed by a foot, nearly taking himself off his cleats.

"Okay," Luis said, stepping out. "Adjustments." The at-bat went on for six pitches. Foul balls, one close take, then a chopper to third. Tyler fielded and flipped to first. Moose caught it in stride.

"One," Moose said, tossing the ball around the horn even though no one had told him to.

Next came Marco. Then Henry. Then the Maple Street brothers, both swinging like they were in their own driveway.

The plays weren't perfect. A throw sailed. A grounder ate up Devon at second. A fly ball fell between two outfielders who both thought the other had it. But something else started to click.

After a missed cutoff, Tyler held his hand up. "That's on me," he said. "I should have been yelling where to go. Next one, listen for my mouth, not your panic."

Kyle, in the other dugout, clapped. "Good," he yelled. "Communication that doesn't sound like a crime scene. We like that."

By the bottom of the second, no one was asking what the score was.

Nobody kept score out loud by then. You could read it off shoulders, dugout noise, and the pace of the warm-up tosses between innings.

But the board beyond right-center stayed blank, its digital red numbers asleep.

Parents on Mute

In the bleachers, the parents watched like they were learning a different sport.

No one had told them not to cheer. They just seemed unsure what volume was allowed at a game that didn't belong to anyone's program.

After a shaky play at second, Tariq kicked at the dirt, annoyed. "You're fine," Henry called from left. "Now you know where the rock is. You got it next time." On the bleachers, Tariq's father shifted.

"That's usually me," he said quietly. "Telling him to shake it off." Karyn smiled.

"Looks like they've got it covered tonight," she said. Tommy sat with his elbows on his knees, chin in his hands. He watched every pitch, every throw, every smile.

"I forget they can do this without us," he said. "You forget you're allowed to let them," Karyn replied. At one point, Devon slid hard into second, throwing up a spray of dirt.

The fielder's tag came down late. Both of them looked up at the umpire who wasn't there.

"Safe," Devon said. "I beat it." The second baseman hesitated.

"Yeah," he said. "You did. My bad. Nice slide." From the bleachers, a few parents instinctively started to react, then checked themselves.

"Did you see that?" one mom said. "They just... fixed it." "Without a Facebook post afterward," another added.

Jack, standing near the fence, heard them and tried not to grin.

The Turn

In the fourth, with the light starting to go soft, Kyle came to the plate with the bases loaded. Two outs. Tie game, whatever that meant tonight.

Tyler toed the rubber. "You want me to throw it where your elbow won't complain about it later?" he called. "Just don't bounce it," Kyle replied. "I like my teeth where they are."

Tyler set, breathed, and delivered a first-pitch curve that didn't quite break. Kyle watched it all the way in and didn't move.

"Ball," he said. "Generous ump," Tyler muttered. He tried again. This time a fastball at the knees. Kyle swung and fouled it straight back, the sound sharp and clean. "Still got it," someone yelled from the dugout.

Two more pitches. Two more fouls. On the fifth, Tyler tried to sneak a changeup past him. Kyle was ready.

He stayed back, hands loose, and shot a line drive into the gap in rightcenter. Two runs scored easily. Tariq, running from first, never stopped, chugging around third, helmet crooked, arms pumping.

The relay came in a split second late. Three runs on a swing that wouldn't show up anywhere official. As Kyle pulled into second, breathless, the kids on his team poured out of the dugout, yelling and laughing. Moose clapped him on the helmet as he walked back to the bag.

"That's what I'm talking about," Moose said. "Old man still has some juice."

Tyler picked up the ball behind the mound and smiled, even as his team fell behind.

"If you tell anyone I'm happy for you," he called, "I'll deny it." "Ledger's got it in ink," Kyle shot back.

Raising a Hand By the sixth, the air had cooled. Lights buzzed fully awake. Bugs gathered in lazy orbits around them.

Tyler's back tightened on a long inning. He'd thrown more pitches than he would have in a carefully monitored academy outing, but the intensity felt different. Less edge, more sweep.

He struck out the first kid on three pitches, then gave up a bloop single, a walk, and a ground ball that should have been a double play but wasn't.

Sweat gathered at his collar. His arm sent him the first quiet signal. Not pain. Just a whisper: That's enough.

In the dugout, Kyle watched his brother's shoulders. He recognized the change. "Call it," he shouted. "Practice what you preach."

Tyler stepped off the back of the mound, ball in hand. Every instinct he'd learned in Elite games told him to wave the coach off, to grind through, to "show toughness."

Instead, he raised his hand. "I'm good," he called to Jack. "But I'm done."

The field went still for half a heartbeat. "Copy that," Jack said. "Who's next?"

A sophomore named Nate—tall, lanky, more enthusiasm than polish —grabbed his glove and sprinted in from left.

"You sure?" he asked Tyler as they passed. "Yeah," Tyler said. "Go make me look smart."

He jogged to third, rolling his shoulder once, feeling the strange mix of relief and pride in doing the thing he'd told younger kids to do a hundred times. On the bleachers, Karyn exhaled, a breath she hadn't realized she'd been holding since April. "Well," she said. "If nothing else, we got our money's worth tonight."

Tommy nodded. "I'm putting this in the ledger," he said. "Under 'things we didn't think we'd see.' " Last Inning They lost track of innings in the best possible way. Someone announced it must be "about the seventh" because the sky over left had gone orange and the first star was stubbornly trying to appear.

"Last ups," Kyle called. "We hit it until someone complains they can't see. Call your own dusk."

They agreed. Everyone nodded. The last half-inning began with a kid who had barely spoken all night. Henry stepped in, bat loose in his hands. He wore no logo. His cleats were scuffed. He'd played left and center and once even trotted in to pitch an inning when no one else wanted it.

Tyler, now at third, looked at him and saw flashes of himself before the numbers. Kyle saw half the kids who had ever walked through the gate.

Henry swung at the first pitch and sent a soft liner over the pitcher's head. It landed just in front of Devon at second and kicked by him into shallow center. The bench erupted like he'd hit it to the parking lot.

"There you go," someone yelled. "Now you're dangerous." Two batters later, Tariq smoked a ball down the line that would have been a double anywhere. Henry scored from second, chugging, helmet askew, a grin splitting his face in a way nobody had seen all summer.

By the time the last out was recorded—a pop-up that Moose caught basket-style at first, trying to make it look cool —the sky had gone navy blue.

"No extras," Kyle called. "We're out of light and good decisions." There was a collective, happy groan.

After No one sprinted off to another field. No one rushed to a recruiting talk or a metrics table. They lingered.

Someone found a half-deflated football under the bleachers and started running routes in right. A cluster of kids sat on the first-base line comparing blisters. Others leaned on the dugout rail, talking about school starting, about drivers' tests, about which teacher gave the least homework.

On the bleachers, parents stretched stiff backs and traded looks that said more than words.

"I wish we had more of these," one said. "We can," another replied. "No one's stopping us but the calendar we keep filling."

At the fence, Jack and Tommy watched Tyler and Kyle walk the infield together, picking up stray balls, smoothing the worst of the cleat marks with their feet.

"That felt... different," Tommy said. Jack nodded.

He glanced at the ledger on the bench. "You going to write it down?" he asked.

Tommy picked up the book, flipped to the page with WHAT WE WON'T SPEND, and then to another where Karyn had started keeping a different kind of record.

He wrote in block letters: Late August 2008 — Spirit Game at Veterans. Seventeen kids. Zero fees. Zero radar readings. One arm raised before it broke. Joy: unqualified yes.

He closed the book softly. Under the Fence As the last of the kids drifted toward the parking lot, Tyler and Kyle walked to the right-field corner.

The carved initials were still there, weathered but legible.

Tyler ran his fingers over them. "Think they'd approve?" he asked. "Of what?" Kyle said.

"Us," Tyler replied. "Tonight. The ledger. All of it." Kyle shrugged.

"Probably they'd just want to know if we left the gate open for the next ones," he said.

He nodded toward the infield where a couple of younger kids were still dragging their feet through the dirt like they didn't want to leave.

Tyler smiled.

"You think we ever get our letters up there?" he asked. "Maybe," Kyle said. "If we earn them."

He thought for a second. "Not for numbers," he added. "For nights like this." They stood there a moment longer, listening to the hum of the highway, the distant thump of bass from some passing car, the quieter sound of kids laughing by the gate.

Jack joined them, hands in his pockets. "Good work, boys," he said.

"Whose idea was it really?" Tyler asked. "Yours or his?" He nodded toward Kyle.

Jack shrugged. "Doesn't matter," he said. "Fence doesn't care whose hand swung the hammer. It just knows whether kids are on the field."

He looked at both of them. "You remember this the next time a program tells you there's only one way to be serious about the game," he said. "You remember tonight. You tell them you've seen another way."

Tyler nodded. "I will," he said.

Kyle rested his palm flat on the fence. "So this is it?" he asked. "The Spirit Game?" Jack smiled.

"One of them," he said. "If we've done our jobs, there will be more. Some you plan. Some just happen when the right kids show up at the right time."

He started toward the shed. "Lights go off in five," he called over his shoulder. "Make sure you get out of here before I lock you in. I'm too old to sleep in the dugout."

Tyler and Kyle walked back across the grass, side by side, cleats whispering on the dirt. When the poles finally clicked off, the field fell into darkness.

The laughter did not. For a few seconds more, you could still hear it— car doors slamming, someone calling, "I got shotgun," the easy rhythm of kids who had, for one night, played a game that didn't need any of the extras to feel big.

Out by the fence, the initials caught the last of the sky's light and then vanished, waiting for whatever came next.

CAMP OFFICE—THE UNWRITTEN OFFER

The coach who asked to meet Jack didn't look like a savior. He looked like a man in a hurry—nice polo, nice watch, eyes that measured before they softened.

"Tyler has tools," the coach said, sitting back in the folding chair. "Not just bat speed. He competes."

Jack nodded, careful. Compliments were currency here. "We could talk about him," the coach continued. "Not official, you understand. But... conversations happen."

Jack felt the old hope rise, hot and dangerous. Then the coach slid a folder across the table. Inside was a brochure for an affiliated training program—branding, packages, a signature line.

"Our guys," the coach said, tapping the page, "they're in a pipeline. It keeps things clean. Keeps parents from... wandering."

Jack looked up. "You want exclusivity." The coach smiled like Jack had said something amusing. "I want commitment," he corrected. "If you're with us, you're with us."

Jack heard the trap: say yes and you're owned; say no and you're ungrateful.

"Tyler's with baseball," Jack said. "That's the only exclusivity he owes." The coach's smile tightened. For a moment, Jack saw the other face beneath it—the one that decided who got calls returned.

"Suit yourself," the coach said lightly. "Just know... other families are willing. And coaches talk."

Jack stood. He forced his hand to be steady as he offered it. The coach shook it with a polite grip that meant nothing.

Outside, Jack found Tyler sitting on a curb, laces undone, sweat drying on his neck. Tyler looked up, searching Jack's face for news.

"How'd it go?" Tyler asked. Jack paused. The man who had known him since he was eight wanted to protect him. The other man — the one who had been honest with George Davis and Mary Davis and never once managed to be otherwise — wanted him to hear it straight, so he wouldn't confuse this world for justice.

"It went," Jack said finally. "And we didn't sell you." Tyler blinked. Relief and anger crossed his face in quick succession. "Maybe we should have," he muttered.

Jack flinched — not at the words, but at what they meant. The machine was inside the boy now, negotiating.

They walked back to the field in silence, both of them carrying the cost of a clean decision.

Chapter Twelve — The Spirit Game

Early Spring 2009 · The Ruggiero Kitchen / Cedarbrook Field

BY THE TIME THE snow finally melted that year, the ledger lived in the middle of the Ruggiero kitchen table like a fifth chair.

It had started as a curiosity—Mary Davis's neat handwriting from another era, columns labeled WHAT WE'LL PAY and WHAT WE WON'T SPEND, little notes about gas and uniforms and light bills. Over the last few months, Karyn's pen had crept in beside Mary's in a darker ink, newer entries woven into the old.

On a raw March night, the wind rattling the storm windows, Tommy dropped a thick envelope onto the table beside the ledger.

RETURNING PLAYER – NORTH SHORE ELITE

SPRING / SUMMER / FALL PROGRAMS

"Draft notice came," he said. Karyn looked up from her shift schedule. Her scrubs still smelled faintly of antiseptic and coffee.

"Already?" she asked. "We just put the Christmas stuff back in the basement."

Tommy slid the pages out. They fanned across the table: program descriptions, color-coded calendars, price breakdowns. Bronze, Silver, Gold again—only now the numbers beside each tier had climbed.

He flipped to the back page. "Total seasonal investment," he read aloud. "Not including travel, lodging, meals, private lessons, or 'optional' showcases." He snorted. "They should just write 'everything you actually end up paying' in parentheses."

Karyn reached for the ledger and opened it to the most recent entries. First tournament: three games, two nights, four hundred and thirty-seven dollars.

Tyler's arm: sore. Kyle's knees: sore. Joy: question mark.

Below that, in her own handwriting, were two more lines. Spirit Game at Veterans: zero fees. Joy: unqualified yes.

She ran her finger under the words once, like reading a prayer. "Tyler's not the same kid he was two years ago," she said quietly. "Kyle either. We're not the same parents. We can't just re-up and hope the costs feel different this time."

Tommy sank into the chair opposite her, rubbing a hand over his face. "I keep thinking about that August night," he said. "The Spirit Game.

Seventeen kids, one field, no invoices. I haven't seen Ty breathe like that before or since."

"And he slept like a human that night," Karyn added. "Not like a forty-year-old construction worker with back problems."

Tommy chuckled, then sobered. "You know what the academy would say," he said. "That the Spirit Game doesn't get him seen. Doesn't build his metrics. Doesn't 'maximize his window.' " Karyn tapped the ledger. "Maybe we stop letting people who send us invoices define what counts," she said.

The wind rattled the window again. Somewhere down the hall, Tyler laughed at something on the television. Kyle's footsteps moved overhead.

"So what are you saying?" Tommy asked. "We walk away? Completely?" Karyn exhaled slowly, eyes on Mary's columns.

"I'm saying we make a plan," she replied. "Our plan. Not theirs." Drawing Lines They pulled their chairs closer to the table until their knees touched, the ledger between them.

"Start with what we know we don't want," Karyn said. "It's easier than pretending everything's on the table."

Tommy nodded. "Okay," he said. "We don't want four straight weekends in hotel rooms." Karyn wrote: Four-weekend tournament runs: NO. "We don't want Tyler pitching twice in a day," she added.

"Under any circumstances. I don't care what's on the line." She wrote: Two outings same day: NO. Tommy thought back to plastic bleachers, July heat, a coach asking Tyler for "one more inning."

"We don't want to spend money on 'exposure events' where the only people watching are other parents and one guy with a camera," he said. "If someone's going to film our kid, they can at least send us the tape."

Karyn smiled and added: Paying for 'exposure' to nobody: NO. They paused. "What about what we keep?" Tommy asked. Karyn turned to a fresh page and wrote at the top: WHAT WE'LL KEEP "Tyler loves to compete," she said. "Really compete. Not in a lobby, not in a metrics lab. On a field. With teammates. He needs some of that."

"So… a team," Tommy offered. "Games that matter. Just not all of them." "We keep lifting," Karyn added. "Strength work. Done right. His body's changing; he needs to build it, not just burn it."

"And the arm care stuff," Tommy said. "The real arm care stuff, not the brochure kind."

Karyn nodded and wrote: A team that plays real games. Thoughtful strength and arm care work. She hesitated, then added: Cedarbrook Field. Tommy watched her underline it. "We keep Jack," she said simply.

"Good," Tommy replied. "That's the only part they can't sell us anyway." They sat back.

"What about the academy?" Tommy asked at last. They both looked at the returner packet spread across the table. "Bronze is basically just a team with their name on it," Karyn said. "Silver is where they start dangling exposure. Gold…" She shook her head. "Gold is tuition."

Tommy flipped through the pages again, seeing the bolded words in a new light.

"What if we don't pick a package?" he said slowly. "What if we take what actually helps and leave the rest?"

Karyn raised an eyebrow. "Are we allowed to do that?" she asked. "I don't know," Tommy answered. "But I'm getting tired of assuming we're not allowed to do anything unless it's on their form."

He tapped the ledger. "This is our form," he said. "Mary's and ours. Maybe it's time we started treating it that way."

The Call

The next afternoon, Tyler found his parents in the same seats at the table, the ledger still open, the academy packet now dog-eared.

"You look like you're about to tell me I'm grounded," he said cautiously. "Not yet," Tommy replied. "Sit down, Ty. We want to talk about this year."

Tyler dropped into the chair between them, eyes flicking from the papers to the ledger to their faces.

"Am I in trouble?" he asked. "No," Karyn said. "We're in... reconsideration." Tommy slid the top page toward him.

"This is what the academy wants from us this year," he said. "Money, time, weekends, your arm."

Tyler skimmed it, not surprised.

"And this," Karyn said, pointing to the ledger, "is what we want for you. For us."

Tyler studied the columns. His own name appeared now in Mary's old book more often than he'd expected—next to season fees, yes, but also next to little notes: Ty asks to throw with Jack on a day off: yes. Ty sleeps through whole night after Spirit Game: yes. "Kyle's been talking to Jack," Tommy said. "We've been talking at work and in parking lots and hospital hallways. None of us like how last summer felt. Not all of it was bad. But too much of it was... wrong-sized."

"Too big?" Tyler asked.

"Too loud," Karyn replied. "Too expensive. Too much pressure in places that don't deserve it, and not enough in the ones that do."

Tyler thought of hotel lobbies and lobby pools. Of games where he had been evaluated more than known.

"What are you thinking?" he asked. "We're not going Gold," Tommy said. "That's off the table. Silver too. We're not buying a package this year."

Tyler opened his mouth. "What if—" he started.

"We're not walking away from your dreams," Karyn cut in gently. "We're just changing vehicles."

Tommy took a breath. "We're going to tell the academy we want roster spots for the summer schedule only," he said. "No mandatory winter program, no metrics showcase, no 'exposure weekends' three states away. You'll play games with good competition, you'll train your body smart, you'll throw with Jack at Veterans, and you'll rest when your arm says rest."

Tyler stared at them. "Are they going to let you do that?" he asked.

"They might not," Tommy said. "They might tell us it's all or nothing. If they do, we'll choose nothing and figure the rest out. You'd play town ball. Fall ball with someone who understands what your elbow is for. We'll find innings that don't require a hotel stamp."

Tyler felt something he hadn't expected: a mix of relief and... fear.

"What if that means I... fall behind?" he asked softly. "What if the kids who do everything get picked and I don't?"

Karyn reached across the table and took his hand. "You're not a stock, Ty," she said. "You don't go up or down based on how many weekends we buy. You're a person. Our person. If a program can't see you unless we swipe a card for every event they offer, maybe they're not the decisionmakers we want in charge of your future."

Tommy added, "The right coaches—the ones who actually matter — will notice the kid who can pitch and compete whether he's got an Elite logo on his sleeve or a town one. Jack's been telling us that for thirty years. We just needed to remember we believed him."

Tyler swallowed.

"And you're really okay with this?" he asked. "With saying no?"

"We're tired of saying yes to everything and then apologizing to ourselves later," Karyn said. "This year, if we say yes, it'll be on purpose."

Tyler looked at the ledger again. The new lines Karyn had written that winter glowed in the overhead light.

He thought of Veterans. Of the Spirit Game. Of the way his chest had felt on the ride home that night—tired and full at the same time.

"Okay," he said finally. "I'm in. Whatever we decide, I'm in." Tommy exhaled like he'd been holding that answer inside his ribs for months.

"Good," he said. "Because I already told Jack we were done plowing the whole family into every event with a logo."

Tyler laughed despite himself. "Of course you did," he said.

Coach Rick

The phone call came that evening. Tommy had rehearsed it three times in his head before he dialed. "Coach Rick, it's Tommy Ruggiero."

"Tommy!" Rick boomed. "I was just looking at your guys' names on my returning list. You all set for a big year? We've got some huge events lined up. Spring Classic, two Perfect Game weekends, Fall Prospect Series—" "That's actually what I'm calling about," Tommy cut in, trying to keep his voice even. "We got the packet. We've been looking it over."

"Great," Rick said. "If you want to lock in a Gold spot, we should do that sooner rather than later. Those always go first."

"We're not going Gold," Tommy said. There was a brief silence on the line.

"Okay," Rick said slowly. "Silver then. Honestly, for a kid like Tyler —" "We're not going Silver either," Tommy said. "We're... rebalancing."

"Rebalancing," Rick repeated, as if tasting a new drill name. "What does that mean?"

"It means we want Tyler to play on a summer roster," Tommy said. "He loves the guys. The competition's good. But we're not signing up for four out-of-state tournaments, the whole winter program, or the metrics showcases. He'll lift at school. He'll throw with our guy here. We'll pick one or two events that make sense and leave the rest."

There was another silence, longer this time. "Tommy," Rick said at last, "I respect what you're trying to do. But you have to understand: at this level, it's all connected. College coaches look at the whole body of work. If Tyler pulls back now, it sends a message."

Tommy tightened his grip on the phone. "What message is that?" he asked. "That we value his arm and his sanity?

That we don't want to spend another summer living in lobbies?"

"That you're not fully committed," Rick said. "College guys talk. They ask us who's all-in. I can't in good conscience tell them a kid is al-l-in if he's cherry-picking events." Tommy felt heat rise in his neck.

"With respect, Coach," he said, "Tyler's been all-in since he was eight years old shagging balls at Veterans. He's pitched when it was forty degrees and when it was ninety-five. He's thrown in front of nobody and in front of guns. He's done every drill you've put in front of him. If taking care of his arm and his family makes us look half-in, maybe the definition needs work."

On the other end, Rick sighed.

"I get it," he said. "I do. I've been on that side of the fence too. But the game's changed. There's a machine to feed."

"We're not interested in feeding the machine," Tommy replied. "We're interested in raising a kid. So here's where we are. If there's room for Tyler on a summer roster under those terms, we're listening. If not, we'll wish you well and find innings somewhere that doesn't require us to sign up for a payment plan to prove we care."

He half-expected an argument. Instead, Rick let out a short, dry laugh. "You're not the first parent to say that this year," he admitted. "You're the first to say it without screaming."

"How'd you answer the others?" Tommy asked. "I told them the same thing I'm going to tell you," Rick said. "We'll find a spot. Kid's too good not to. But I can't promise him the same exposure. He won't be on the videos we cut from the top events. He might miss a 'look' here or there."

"If the right coach wants him, he'll find him in a box score or a dusty field as easily as he will on a highlight reel," Tommy said. "We'll take our chances."

Rick was quiet for a beat, then said, softer, "You know, when I started this thing, we only had one team. We played twenty games in a summer and half of them were at places like your Cedarbrook Field. No banners. Just good dirt."

"What happened?" Tommy asked. Rick didn't answer the question directly. "I'll send you the revised schedule," he said instead. "You pick two tournaments that make sense. We'll build the rest around the local league. Tell Tyler I expect him to compete his butt off in the ones he shows up to. If we're doing less, we're going to do it better."

"That's what we want," Tommy said. "Thanks, Coach." When he hung up, he had the relief of a pitcher finally shaking off the wrong sign.

The New Rhythm Spring settled in fits and starts. Tyler still lifted before school, still threw bullpens, still ran poles in the outfield when nobody else was watching. But the calendar on the fridge looked different.

Two tournaments circled instead of six. More blank weekends. A handful of nights with VETERANS in Karyn's handwriting instead of ELITE in printed type.

On the first truly warm Wednesday, they walked down to the field together — Tommy, Karyn, Tyler, and Kyle — carrying a bucket of balls and a bag of mismatched practice jerseys. Jack was already there, of course, dragging the infield.

"Thought you'd forgotten where this place was," he called.

"GPS still works," Tommy answered. Tyler jogged ahead. Kyle joined Marco and Luis near shortstop. More kids trickled in — some academy, some rec, some whose cleats had seen more driveway than turf.

Later that night, after the boys had showered and the house had gone mostly quiet, Karyn sat at the table with the ledger open and added a new line. Spring 2009 — New plan: two tournaments, more Veterans, less noise.

She closed the book and turned off the kitchen light.

Chapter Thirteen — Tyler at the Fence

,

THE WORST PART WASN'T the inning. It was the screenshot.

Somebody's dad had filmed the game on their phone and clipped the worst thirty seconds.

A walk. A hanging breaking ball that got hammered into the gap.

Another walk. By the time the coach came to get Tyler with the bases loaded, the student-run Twitter account for the league had already pushed out the final line: Tyler Ruggiero (Saugus): 1.1 IP, 3 H, 4 ER, 3 BB, 1 K. "Rough one for the Elite righty tonight," the caption read.

Nobody mentioned the inning before, when he'd carved through the heart of the order. Nobody mentioned the strikeout on a fastball that popped the mitt just right. Nobody mentioned the ground ball that should have been a double play if the second baseman hadn't kicked it.

The scoreboard didn't care about context. Neither did the internet.

Two days later, the Academy put up a new board on the wall. White. Glossy. Full of names.

NORTH SHORE ELITE — SUMMER LEADERBOARD

Columns marched across the top like a report card: FB Velo · Top Exit Velo · Sixty Time · Hard Hit % · K/BB Ratio. Tyler found his name halfway down. Fastball: 83. Sixty: 7.4. Exit velo: "pending."

A kid he'd never seen before, from somewhere west of 128, sat near the top. Fastball: 87. Sixty: 6.9.

"Four D1s already DM'd me," the new kid said loudly in the cage. "Coach says if I hit 90 by next summer, I'm on the national radar."

Tyler nodded. He stared at the board and did the math he'd learned to do in his head.

If I'm 83 now and I add two or three a year... if I clean up my mechanics... if I live in the weight room... He'd gone from loving numbers— RBI, batting average, pitch counts — to feeling like they were a language he could never speak quite fluently enough.

On the drive home, the numbers followed him. 83. 7.4.

1.1 IP, 4 ER. "You okay?" Tommy asked at a red light. "Yeah," Tyler said. Reflex. Tommy glanced over.

"Try again." Tyler let his breath out, long and frayed. "I don't even know what I'm trying to win anymore," he said. "I battled back from the bad outing. I did everything Jack says to do. But the only numbers anybody posts are the ones that make it look like I don't belong."

He swallowed. "Feels like the scoreboard's always losing, even when I'm not." They pulled up to the house and sat there for a moment with the engine ticking.

"You free tomorrow?" Tommy asked. "Yeah. No games." "Good," Tommy said. "We're going to Veterans. Jack texted. Says it's time to talk about a different kind of scoreboard."

The Old Board

The next afternoon, Cedarbrook Field was between games. No league scheduled, no organized practice. Just that familiar hush it got when it was waiting.

Jack was already there, of course.

He stood near the third-base dugout, wrestling a wooden frame out of the storage shed. It was about the size of the Academy leaderboard, but that was where the resemblance ended.

The wood was old, edges worn soft. The center was a sheet of slate, black and dull. Faded chalk clung to it in ghost letters: HITS RUNS ERRORS "Thought we'd retired that thing," Tommy said, grabbing one end. "We did," Jack said. "Until I saw the picture of that new wall you sent me."

He nodded toward the fence. "Let's hang it up here for a bit."

They set the frame on two old sawhorses by the backstop. Jack wiped at the slate with the side of his hand, smearing the old words into a gray blur.

"Keeps showing up," he said. "Different fonts, different logos, same problem."

Tyler dropped his bag and came closer. "What problem?" he asked.

Jack nodded toward Tommy's phone, where the Academy board glowed in miniature. "Velocity. Exit velo. Sixty times. All useful," he said. "None of them a full story." He flipped open the small notebook he seemed to keep half his life in.

"So we're going to build you another board," he said. "One the internet doesn't get to share. One the Academy can't erase."

Categories Jack wrote for a minute, then handed the notebook to Tyler. At the top, in block letters:

FENCE SCOREBOARD—TYLER Underneath, a simple list:

Showed Up (Y/N) Effort (0–3) Focus (0–3) Body Care (0–3) Helped Someone Else (Y/N) Learned Something New (Y/N) Loved the Game (0–3) Impact (0–3) "Doesn't look like any scoreboard I've ever seen," Tyler said. "Good," Jack said. "Those ones aren't doing the job."

He went through the categories, but he didn't lecture. Showed Up was either yes or no. Effort was zero to three, no decimals. Focus was the same. Body Care — did you warm up, do your bands, shut it down when your arm said so, or did you treat your shoulder like a rental car? On Helped Someone Else he stayed a beat longer than the others.

"Did you leave somebody better than you found them?" he said. "A younger kid, a teammate, some twelve-year-old who's never stood on this dirt before. If the answer is no for too many days in a row, we've got bigger problems than velocity."

He paused on the last one.

"Loved the Game. That's the sneaky big category. Zero means you hated every second. One means you tolerated it. Two means you're glad you came. Three means you leave with more joy than you arrived with. You're allowed zeros. We just don't want them stacking up like bad debt."

He handed Tyler the chalk. "Pick a day. Any day. Let's score it."

Tyler thought back to the outing with the ugly line on Twitter.

"Yesterday," he said.

They scored it together. Some categories Tyler called for himself; Body Care Jack made him drop a number on, because he'd ignored his arm telling him it was cooked and thrown thirty pitches in one frame anyway. The scoring took ten minutes and felt longer.

When they were done, the line held good news and bad. Tyler frowned at it.

"That still isn't a win," he said.

Jack pointed at the Twitter line Tommy had printed and taped to the bottom of the frame. 1.1 IP, 3 H, 4 ER, 3 BB, 1 K.

"Compared to this?" Jack asked. "You tell me which one tells you more about who you were that day."

Tyler looked from one to the other. Both stung. One closed a door. The other pointed toward one.

"If I see this," Jack said, tapping the Fence Scoreboard, "I see a kid who showed up, worked, lost his focus for a bit, ignored his own fatigue, helped people anyway, learned something, and didn't let one bad inning kill the whole season in his head. That kid? I can build with him."

He tapped the Twitter line. "That one just tells me the ball found some barrels."

Tyler let his breath out slowly.

"So you're saying I can lose an inning and still win the day," he said.

"Exactly," Jack said. "Start stacking enough won days and the big numbers usually take care of themselves."

The Other Kids

Word got out slowly. Not because Jack advertised anything. Because kids talk.

"Ruggiero's been down at Veterans a lot," somebody said one night at the Academy. "Not just with Jack. With little dudes too."

"Yeah, my cousin went there," another kid said. "Said Tyler worked with him for like half an hour. Didn't charge him or anything."

"Why would he?" someone else snorted. "He's not a coach." "He kind of was," the cousin said.

On a humid July afternoon, two younger players showed up while Tyler and Jack were already in the middle of a session.

One was a lanky fourteen-year-old with a stiff delivery and a fastball he wanted "to get seen."

The other was twelve and hopelessly earnest, with a glove that still creaked when he closed it.

"You guys mind if we hit on the side?" the older one asked. "Coach Rick said if we're going to do extra work, this is a good place."

Jack looked at Tyler. "Your field too," he said quietly. "You want to share it?" Tyler thought about his notebook. Helped Someone Else (Y/N). "Yeah," he said. "Let's run stations."

He spent twenty minutes with the older boy in the shade of the dugout, watching video on a phone, showing him how to feel his back leg instead of just leaning toward the plate.

Then he turned to the twelve-year-old. "What do you want to get out of today?" Tyler asked.

The kid thought hard. "I want to not be scared of ground balls," he said. "And I want to hit one hard enough that it scares somebody else."

Tyler grinned. "That's a good list," he said. "We can work with that." They set up short-hop drills, then simple front toss. Every time the kid flinched and stayed with it anyway, Tyler heard Jack in his head.

Impact. By the time the sun slid behind the right-field trees, the little one had taken a bad hop off the chest, laughed, and asked for another. The older one had felt one pitch come out easier than any he'd thrown all summer.

On the walk back to the lot, Tyler flipped open the notebook. Showed Up: Y Effort: 3 Focus: 3 Body Care: 3 Helped Someone Else: Y Learned Something New: Y (how to teach back-leg load) Impact: 3 Loved the Game: 3 "For the record," Jack said, peeking over his shoulder, "that's a blowout."

Jack's Story

One evening, when the light thinned early and the air started to smell like school again, Jack closed up the shed and sat on the bleachers next to Tyler.

"You know why I make such a big deal about this scoreboard stuff?" he asked. "Because the internet's stupid?" Tyler guessed.

Jack huffed a laugh. "Partly," he said. "Mostly because I spent a long time letting the wrong board tell me who I was."

He looked out at the field instead of at Tyler. "When I was your age, numbers were everything," he said. "Hits.

ERA. That little column in the paper. I chased them like they were the only keys to any door. Made some teams. Missed some others.

Thought I was worth something when they were good. Thought I was nothing when they weren't."

He rubbed his thumb along the seam of a baseball. "Then life happened," he said. "Jobs. Bills. Losses you don't come back from in nine innings. Turns out, none of those box scores mattered nearly as much as I thought. What did matter was how I showed up when nobody was keeping stats."

He tapped the notebook in Tyler's lap.

"You've got a chance to learn that while you're still playing," he said. "To let this stuff carry more weight than some guy with a logo's opinion of your arm."

He smiled, lines deepening around his eyes. "And here's the funny part," he added. "Players who live by this scoreboard? They usually end up with better numbers on the other one anyway. They stop gripping the bat like it's their permanent record."

Tyler watched the way the late light made the grass glow. "You think this will really matter when college coaches start calling?" he asked.

"Depends which ones," Jack said. "The ones worth playing for will see it. Not on a stat sheet. In how you walk. In how you respond when you give up a bomb. In how you treat the bullpen catcher on a ninety--five-degree day."

He looked at Tyler. "They may not know what to call it," he said. "But they'll feel it." Kitchen Table The first time a college coach called, it happened on a random Tuesday night in the middle of folding laundry.

Tommy nearly dropped the phone. Karyn mouthed, Who is it? even though she already knew from the way his eyes went wide.

Tyler came in from the driveway with his glove still in his hand, breathing a little harder than a simple game of catch should have required.

"Coach from Stonefield," Tommy said, covering the receiver. "Wants to talk to you."

They sat him at the kitchen table like he was interviewing for a job. He stumbled through the first few answers, then found his footing. Yes, sir. No, sir. I'm working on my changeup. Grades are good. Yes, I know nothing's guaranteed. Yes, sir, I'm willing to compete.

When the call ended, he leaned back, cheeks flushed, eyes bright and dazed.

"That just happened," he said. Tommy grinned. Karyn smiled too, though her hand went automatically to Tyler's elbow, feeling along the tendons like she could read the future in them.

Later that night, when the house had quieted, Karyn found the notebook on the counter, open to a fresh page.

She sat down and read the lines. Showed Up (Y/N) Effort (0–3) Focus (0–3) Body Care (0–3) Helped Someone Else (Y/N) Learned Something New (Y/N) Loved the Game (0–3) Impact (0–3) The day's entry sat beneath in Tyler's uneven block letters. Showed Up: Y Effort: 3 Focus: 3 Body Care: 3 Helped Someone Else: Y (talked freshman through pregame routine) Learned Something New: Y (first time handling college coach conversation) Loved the Game: 3 Impact: 3 Karyn traced the last line with her thumb. "In ten years," she said when Tyler wandered back into the kitchen for a glass of water, "this will tell me more about who you were than whatever numbers sit on some frozen website."

She closed the notebook gently. "Still want to chase the other scoreboard?" she asked. Tyler nodded.

"Yeah," he said. "I still want to see how good I can get. I still want a shot at college ball."

He glanced toward the living room, where a game flickered on the TV, then back at his mother. "But I don't want that to be the only board I read," he said. "Or the only one you judge me by." Jack, who had stopped by for coffee and stayed for the conversation, smiled.

"Good," he said. "Because those other ones? They get turned off. Seasons end. Websites crash. Programs change staffs. This one"—he tapped the notebook—"sticks."

The Field's Score

On the last truly warm evening of that fall, Tyler walked down to Veterans alone. No scheduled session. No text from Jack. No plan.

He just showed up. He stood on the mound in the fading light and listened. The field didn't speak in numbers.

It spoke in echoes. The thump of balls in mitts from a hundred prior bullpens. Laughter from the Spirit Game.

The slap of Kyle's glove on the day his knees finally felt strong again. Marco's whoop when he turned his first clean double play.

The quiet murmur of Jack's voice along the fence, teaching some new terrified twelve-year-old how to breathe.

Tyler walked off the back of the mound and into the grass. The old manual scoreboard frame still leaned on its sawhorses by the backstop, slate stained but clean.

He opened the notebook and wrote. Showed Up: Y Effort: 2 Focus: 3 Body Care: 3 Helped Someone Else: N (just me today) Learned Something New: Y (field sounds different when it's this quiet) Loved the Game: 3 Impact: 2 He closed the cover and tucked it under his arm. At the fence, the old carvings waited.

He ran his thumb under them, the way he had on the night they'd first talked about putting his own initials there someday.

"Maybe it won't ever say T. R. up here," he said softly. "Maybe it will. Either way... I'm alright."

The boards, being boards, said nothing. But the field behind them felt like it exhaled.

He picked up a ball and stood just in front of the mound. No radar gun. No cameras. No crowd. Just a boy and a target.

He threw until he couldn't quite see the seams anymore, then stayed for one more pitch anyway, just to feel the motion.

As the last bit of light bled out over the trees, Tyler walked off the field, cleats leaving faint, familiar marks on the dirt.

No one recorded the night. No stat line appeared online. The only scoreboard that changed was the one in his notebook and the one he carried in his chest.

In the years ahead, as recruiting calls came and went, as teammates transferred and coaches changed, as some dreams shrank and others grew in unexpected directions, the Fence Scoreboard would be the one constant.

The place Tyler Ruggiero kept his truest stats. Not for scouts. Not for social media. For himself.

And for the old man at the fence who had taught him that the only scoreboard that really mattered was the one he would still recognize long after the last uniform hung in the back of a closet.

Chapter Fourteen — Saying No

THE EMAIL SUBJECT LINE didn't mess around. SUBJECT: NATIONAL TRACK ROSTER INVITE— CONFIDENTIAL (Tyler Ruggiero) It landed in Tommy's inbox at 6:12 a.m., wedged between a hardware-store sale and a reminder from the electric company.

He almost deleted it as spam. Then he saw the sender. From: Coach Rick—North Shore Elite His stomach did the small, familiar flip of a man who's learned that some messages arrive already carrying a bill.

He tapped it open. Ruggiero Family, I'm excited to extend Tyler an invitation to join our North Shore Elite National Track for the upcoming season. This is our highest-level, invite-only group and represents what we believe to be the top prospects in our program. National Track players receive priority roster placement at premier events up and down the East Coast, as well as guaranteed inclusion at the region's most heavily scouted showcases.

This is a can't-miss opportunity for families serious about maximizing their son's exposure... Tommy's eyes snagged on the phrase can'tmiss. Whoever had written the copy knew exactly what they were doing.

Can't-miss implied only one kind of failure: saying no. He skimmed the rest. Bullet points. Premier events. Discounts that still made his chest tighten. A sign-off that promised they'd "follow up soon."

He looked at the timestamp again. 6:12 a.m. Like they wanted the fear waiting with the coffee.

Karyn padded into the kitchen a few minutes later, hair pulled up, robe cinched, eyes not ready for daylight.

"Morning," she muttered. "Depends how you define it," he said. He slid the phone across the table.

She read the subject line. Then the body. Her jaw ticked once on the words can't-miss and top prospects.

"Of course," she said quietly. "Of course they'd come calling now." Tyler had pitched well. Really well. High school coaches were asking about him. A couple of parents had started throwing around words like projectable at the fence.

"They're not wrong," Tommy said. "He probably could hang at that level."

"Level of play, sure," Karyn said. "Level of schedule? Level of expectation? Level of 'we own your weekends from now until graduation'?"

She handed the phone back like it was buzzing. "What's the actual commitment?" she asked.

"Six big events," Tommy said, repeating what Rick had told him on the phone. "Two down south. Fall league. Two nights a week in the cages all winter. 'Recommended' strength sessions. National guys get invited to the Harbor Stadium showcase, not just the in-house stuff."

He turned the screen so they were both looking at the same three lines. Top prospects. Premier events. Maximum exposure. "I can hear my dad," Tommy said. " 'You'd be an idiot to pass this up. You want the kid to go to college, don't you?' " Karyn didn't answer right away. "We wouldn't have to do all of it," Tommy tried. "We could say yes to National but still protect some weekends. Pick our spots."

"We said that before," Karyn reminded him. "Before the ledger. Before Kyle's elbow. Before we learned how to spell 'tear' in a way we never wanted to learn."

She pulled Mary's ledger out from under the coffee maker and opened it to the dog-eared page.

The lines they'd written months earlier looked back at them in ink that hadn't faded at all.

- No playing through real pain.
- Family gets first claim on weekends some of the time.
- We will not buy the lie that behind on somebody's list = behind in life.

Beside it sat the smaller notebook, the one Karyn had labeled Fence Scoreboard in block letters. No runs or hits in its columns — just three headings: Loved the Game · Healthy Enough · Impact.

She flipped to the most recent week. "Ty's been happy," she said. "Tired, but for the right reasons. These numbers have been twos and threes for months. I like that kid."

"I like him too," Tommy said. "I also don't want to be the dad who has to look him in the eye in three years and say, 'Sorry, we turned down your shot.' " "There's the fear," Karyn said softly. "I was wondering when it would show up."

They let the word sit between them. Fear. "Maybe we ask the people who've actually seen the end of this road," she said. "Not the ones selling tickets to get on it."

"Jack," Tommy said. "And maybe Coach Reilly, if he'll pick up the phone," Karyn added. "The college guy who said he trusts his eyes more than someone's website."

She closed the ledger. "Either way," she said, "we don't answer today. Fear emails get at least one sleep."

* * *

Coach Rick's email turned out to be the soft hand. The hard hand arrived three days later, in a voice they had not heard before.

The laptop fan whined like it was tired of being asked to care. Karyn sat at the kitchen table in her sweatshirt, hair twisted up, a mug cooling beside the mouse. The house was quiet except for the dryer thumping and the tick of the same clock that had watched Jack's generation learn how to lose with grace.

On the screen, the registration page had a timer in the corner. RESERVE YOUR SPOT—00:12:44.

Tyler padded in with a ball in his hand, still in socks, cheeks pink from the cold he'd let in through the back door.

"Dad said we could throw," he whispered, as if the computer might hear him. Karyn's cursor hovered over a box that said I AGREE TO ALL TERMS AND FEES. Beneath it, smaller: ALL PAYMENTS NONREFUNDABLE. A phone number sat at the bottom like an escape hatch that wasn't real.

"In a minute," she said, and hated the way it came out. Tyler waited. He bounced the ball once against his palm. It made a small sound, the sound of play asking to be chosen.

The fees were itemized: winter training package, tournament deposit, uniform set, evaluation fee.

Every line ended in a number. The total at the bottom didn't blink.

From the other room, Tommy's voice carried through the wall—low, careful. Work voice.

"I can't stay late again," he said into the phone. "I already swapped shifts. No, I'm not asking—I'm telling you what I can do."

Karyn stared at the timer. Ten minutes. Then nine. Her phone buzzed. A text from an unknown number:

LAST TWO SPOTS. COACH WANTS TYLER ON THIS ROSTER. DON'T LET THIS SLIP.

She pictured the sideline looks. The whispered, You didn't sign him up? The way mothers said opportunity like it was oxygen.

Tyler rolled the ball gently toward her. It bumped her chair leg and stopped. Karyn's finger moved toward the checkbox.

Then she looked at Tyler's face—open, hopeful, still believing adults made choices for reasons that made sense.

She closed the laptop. The timer vanished with a soft click. For a moment she stood still while the world kept sliding without her.

Tyler blinked. "We're not doing it?" Karyn swallowed. Her throat was tight with all the things she couldn't explain to a kid who still thought a field was a field.

"We're throwing," she said. "Right now." She stood, pulled her sweatshirt tighter, and opened the back door. Cold air rushed in like a dare.

As they stepped into the yard, her phone buzzed again. A voicemail this time. She didn't listen yet. She didn't let the machine speak first.

At North Shore Elite, the lights never asked permission. The facility smelled of rubber pellets and cologne. A row of banners hung above the turf like commandments:

COMMIT. COMPETE. EARN.

Coach Carver sat at a folding table with a clipboard and a laptop, the glow reflecting off the plastic of his staff ID. On the screen was a spreadsheet of names. Next to each: a number, a rank, a note.

He wasn't cruel. That was what made him dangerous. Carver believed—truly believed—that he was saving kids from being overlooked.

He'd been overlooked once himself. Too small. Too late. Too forgettable. He carried that old dismissal like a splinter, and he couldn't stand to watch another boy live inside it.

He clicked on Tyler's row. Under NOTES he typed: strong arm; coachable; father hesitant; mother anxious; leverage: roster timing.

A trainer walked by and nodded toward the bullpen mound. "Kid's elbow again," the trainer said. "Not bad. But if he throws today, it'll bark tomorrow."

Carver didn't flinch. "Every kid's elbow barks," he said.

He glanced at the posted policy taped to the table:

INJURIES MUST BE REPORTED. CLEARANCE REQUIRED. MISSED EVENTS MAY AFFECT ROSTER STATUS.

Policy was his sanctuary. It let him sound professional instead of predatory. His phone rang. Tommy.

Carver answered on the first ring. "Tommy. I was just looking at Tyler's numbers."

Tommy didn't say hello. "We're not sure about the travel weekend." Carver leaned back, letting the chair creak—a tiny performance of patience. "I get it," he said. "Gas isn't cheap. Hotels aren't cheap. Life isn't cheap."

He made his voice warm. Persuasive. The voice of a man offering a ladder. "But here's the truth," Carver continued. "The coaches who matter are there. If Tyler isn't, someone else is. And once a roster sets, it sets. I don't make that rule. I just live in it."

Tommy's breath came through the line, held too long. "He's fifteen," he said finally.

Carver's eyes softened. He could do tenderness too. "And he's good," he replied. "Good enough that he shouldn't get punished because adults are afraid of the bill."

There it was—fear, turned into accusation, dressed as opportunity. Carver lowered his voice. "Listen. I'm not trying to push. I'm trying to protect him. This is how it works now."

He paused, then added the temptation, the one that always landed. "If you want me to hold his spot, I can. But I need the deposit by midnight. After that, the system releases it. Not me."

He hung up and stared at the spreadsheet again. The names sat there like they were already facts.

Across the turf, a boy swung too hard and his bat clanged off the cage frame. The sound rang out.

Carver wrote one more note under Tyler's name. pressure point: deadline.

That night, Tommy and Karyn sat at the edge of their bed with the phone between them like a third person.

The voicemail light blinked. Tommy pressed play.

Carver's voice filled the room, calm and reasonable. Midnight. Deposit. System. Opportunity.

When it ended, the silence felt accusatory. Tommy rubbed his forehead. "He makes it sound like we're the problem." Karyn's hands were clenched in the blanket. "He makes it sound like Tyler will be the one who pays."

Tommy looked at her. "And he will," he said, because he was honest, and honesty in a marriage could sometimes feel like an injury.

Karyn's eyes shone. "So we just... do whatever they want forever?" Tommy didn't answer right away. His gaze went to the closet, to the row of uniforms, to the bag by the door already half packed with the things their family carried to be considered serious.

Karyn's voice softened, and that softness was the most dangerous thing of all. "When do we get him back?" she asked.

Tommy's throat tightened. He loved her. He loved their boys. He loved the version of himself who thought doing everything meant protecting them.

"If we say no," he said, "they'll talk. The parents will talk. Tyler will hear it." Karyn nodded once. "And if we say yes," she replied, "he'll learn the machine owns us."

Tommy stared at the phone. He could feel the weight of the job, the bills, the small humiliations of being the family that couldn't keep up. He could also feel something else—a line inside him that wanted to be straight again.

He reached for Karyn's hand. "If we do this," he said, "we do it together. No blaming. No quiet resentments."

Karyn squeezed back, her grip fierce. "And if it costs us friends?" Tommy looked up. "Then it costs us friends," he said. He felt the words land like a stake driven into dirt.

Karyn leaned in and kissed him. It wasn't comfort. It was a pact. Tommy picked up the phone and deleted the voicemail.

Then he opened the bedside drawer and pulled out the envelope with the check he had written hours earlier, back when his hand was faster than his heart.

He tore it in half. In the morning they would live with what it cost. But that night, for the first time in a long time, they were not paying to make the fear feel organized.

***

Tyler Hears

They didn't make it to the next night. Tyler found out about the invite the way most teenagers find out about everything.

Through someone else's phone. "Dude," Moose said at practice, eyes wide. "You going National?" Tyler blinked. "What?"

"Coach Rick was talking to my dad," Moose said. "He said he's really excited you're on the short list. Said you're a 'National Track arm.' My dad was like, 'That's huge for him.' " National Track.

The words didn't feel real at first. They'd always been something other kids did—kids from bigger towns, wealthier zip codes, places with more fields and fewer cracked driveways.

National kids got the gear first. Their names showed up in posts. They were the ones people whispered about.

By the time Tyler got home, his grip on the steering wheel matched the tight feeling under his ribs. At dinner, he tried to act normal.

He failed.

"What's up?" Kyle asked, shoveling potatoes. "Nothing," Tyler said, staring at his plate.

Karyn and Tommy traded a look. Tommy set down his fork. "So," he said. "Apparently confidentiality isn't a strong suit over at the Academy." Tyler's fork stopped halfway to his mouth.

"You know?" he asked. "About the National Track invite?" Tommy said. "Yeah. We were going to talk tonight. After we had our own panic attack first."

Tyler's cheeks flushed. "So... is it real?" he asked. "Like, actually real?" "It's real," Karyn said. "They want you on that roster." Every part of him lit up and locked up at the same time. "That's... big," he said.

"It is," Tommy agreed. "So is what comes with it." He pushed Mary's ledger and the Fence Scoreboard notebook gently onto the table between them. "We're not going to decide this without you," he said. "But we're also not going to decide it only based on fear. So—before I say anything— tell us what you want." Tyler stared at the wood grain.

"I want to play against good kids," he said slowly. "I want to see how far I can go. I want to end up at a place where I belong, not just a place with a name. And I want to still like baseball when I'm done."

He swallowed. "I also... I don't want to wreck my arm," he added. "And I don't want Kyle to feel like his stuff doesn't matter because mine's louder."

Kyle looked up, surprised. "Wow," Tommy said. "That was pretty much my list too. I just would've added 'I'd like your brother to still have a functioning elbow at thirty.' " Tyler laughed despite himself. "So what do we do?" he asked.

"We take tomorrow," Karyn said. "We talk to Jack. Maybe Coach Reilly. Then we decide. Together."

She looked at both boys. "And we accept that whatever we choose, something will be lost," she said. "The goal is to make sure what we gain is worth it."

Fence Counsel

Jack listened to the whole thing from his usual spot along the backstop, arms folded, cap low, eyes on the infield.

He nodded sometimes. Huffed once. But he didn't interrupt. When Tommy finished recounting the email, the call, and Tyler's reaction, Jack shrugged.

"Of course they invited you," he said to Tyler. "You're good and you're not a pain. Programs love that combo."

"So we should say yes?" Tyler asked, a little too quickly. "I didn't say that," Jack replied. "I said I'm not surprised." He shifted, finally turning to look Tyler full in the face.

"You asking me if you're good enough to be on that team?" he asked. "Yeah," Tyler said.

"You're good enough," Jack said. "That's not the question."

He looked at Tommy and Karyn. "You asking me whether National Track guarantees anything?" he said. "Feels like it," Tommy admitted. "When they call it 'can't-miss'..." Jack snorted.

"Nothing in this game is can't-miss," he said. "Not at fourteen. Not at eighteen. Not at twenty-two when the draft calls — or doesn't."

He pushed off the fence and walked a few steps toward the mound, hands in his pockets. Then he looked back at Tyler.

"If you didn't have this field, I might say go," he said. "You've got a place to fail without it ruining you. Not many kids your age can say that."

Tyler scratched at the edge of the bench with his thumbnail.

"What if I want to go anyway," he said.

"Then you go," Jack said.

"What if I don't."

Jack's mouth tugged. "Then you don't."

He sat down beside Tyler on the bench. He didn't say anything for a while. Tyler kept scratching the bench. The thumbnail caught a sliver and a piece came up. He flicked it away.

"I don't know," Tyler said.

"I know," Jack said. "That's a perfectly good answer for a Wednesday."

The College Voice, Again

That night, after dinner, Tommy stepped out onto the back porch and called. The line clicked.

"Coach Reilly," came the voice. "How's Saugus treating you?"

"Can't complain," Tommy said. "Got a question for you." He laid it out: the email, the schedule, the sales pitch, Tyler's hopes, their fears.

Reilly listened the way good coaches do—quietly, with the occasional small noise that let you know he was still there.

When Tommy finished, there was a pause. "First off," Reilly said, "congrats to the kid. If a good program thinks he's a top guy, that tells me he's doing something right."

"Appreciate that," Tommy said. "We're proud of him." "Second," Reilly said, "let me say this as clearly as I can: I don't care if a kid was on the National Team, the Super-Duper Elite, or the Backyard Bandits. I care if he can play, if he can handle a bad inning, and if he still likes the game enough to be coachable in February."

Tommy let his shoulders drop a half-inch. "So it's not a deal-breaker if he doesn't do this?" he asked. "Not for me," Reilly said. "Look, I'm not naïve. There are places where being on the right list with the right logo helps. It can get my eyes on a kid sooner. But it doesn't keep my eyes there if the kid's miserable or breaking down."

He shifted, the sound of his chair creaking over the line. "When I see 'National Track' on a profile," he said, "I think, 'Okay, someone liked him.' Then I watch him throw. I watch how he reacts when something goes wrong. I watch how he treats his catcher. That matters more than what brand name's across his chest."

Tommy laughed, a little choked.

"So if we don't say yes, we're not slamming every door?" he asked. "You're slamming exactly zero doors," Reilly said. "Worst case? He plays for a good local team, ends up at a good school, and twenty years from now he's got two functioning shoulders and mostly good memories. That's not exactly failure."

He paused. "Whatever you decide," he added, "make sure your son knows it's the schedule you're choosing, not his worth. I've seen too many kids confuse those two and walk away bitter."

"Thank you, Coach," Tommy said. "Tell Ty to keep winning days, not just games," Reilly replied. "That's the stuff that lasts."

The No

They wrote the email together. Tyler sat at the table with his parents, Fence Scoreboard notebook open beside Mary's ledger.

Tommy typed. Coach Rick, Thank you for thinking of Tyler for the National Track roster. We're honored you see him as a player who could compete at that level, and we appreciate all you and your staff have done for him.

After a lot of thought, we've decided to decline the invitation this year. As a family, we're prioritizing a slightly lighter travel load, continued focus on his high school program, and making sure both our boys stay healthy and still love the game.

This isn't a reflection on the program or the opportunity. It's about what we believe is the right balance for Tyler and our family at this time.

We hope he can continue to train and play with North Shore Elite in a way that aligns with this approach.

Thanks again for your belief in him. – Tommy and Karyn Ruggiero Tommy hovered over the send button. "You sure?" he asked.

Tyler took a breath. He thought for a long second. "I don't want to say yes because I'm scared," he said.

Tommy clicked. The whoosh of the email leaving sounded too quiet for how big the decision felt. The reply came that evening.

Totally understand. We're disappointed but respect your decision. The door's always open if you change your mind.

There was no follow-up call. No plea. Just the faint digital echo of a door swinging half-shut. The difference showed up in smaller ways.

Fewer texts from Rick. Fewer "We'd love to see Ty at this" messages. A little more space in the bleacher conversations when Karyn sat down. The silence didn't roar.

It dripped. A cooler tone here. A missed invite there. The slow recalibration of who was "in" and who had stepped to the edges. At home, doubt crept in on quiet nights.

"Did we screw this up?" Tommy asked more than once, staring at the ledger.

Karyn would tap the lines. "No playing through real pain." "Family gets first claim on weekends some of the time." "We will not buy the lie that behind on somebody's list = behind in life." Then she'd open the Fence Scoreboard.

Loved the Game: 3, 3, 2, 3. Healthy Enough: 3, 3, 3, 2. Impact: 3. "If we're wrong," she'd say, "we're wrong in a direction I can live with."

The First Weekend

The first big National Track weekend came in late spring. Social media lit up — kids in crisp uniforms under stadium lights, hashtags about grinding and chasing dreams, hotel lobby photos. Saturday morning, while National warmed up three states away, Tyler and Kyle pulled on plain T-shirts and walked down to Veterans. Jack was already there, dragging the infield. They played until the light went.

That night, Tommy sat at the kitchen table with the Fence Scoreboard and wrote: National Weekend — we were here. We chose something. Something did not leave us.

A Small Confirmation

A week later, at a regular-season high school game, Tyler toed the rubber in front of a modest crowd and a single folding chair with a college pullover draped over it.

Middle of the third, during a mound visit, his coach stepped in close. "See that guy down the line?" he asked.

Tyler nodded. "D3 from up north," the coach said. "Good school. I told him about you. He said he's seen the National boys three times this month. Wanted to see someone who wasn't in that circus." Tyler blinked. "He said that?"

"His words," the coach said. "Not mine. 'Show me a kid who can pitch and still likes the game, not one who's been on a showcase treadmill since ten.' " He clapped Tyler's shoulder. "Now quit listening to me and get this hitter out," he said. Tyler did.

That night, Karyn opened the ledger to the page she'd marked Big Decisions and added a new line. Saying No to National. Beside it, in smaller letters: We'll see.

She closed the book and slid it back where Mary's ledger lived.

Later, Tommy sat alone at the field, Fence Scoreboard open on his knee, the lights humming overhead. The outfield was empty. The fence, as always, held its line.

Loved the Game: 3. Healthy Enough: 3. Impact: 3.

Under "Notes" he wrote: National doesn't text much anymore. That's okay. The field still does.

BLEACHERS—RAIN STARTING

The rumor traveled faster than the schedule: the Ruggieros are pulling out. By the time the story crossed the parking lot, it had already swollen. They weren't leaving baseball. They were skipping one tournament that charged like a ransom and called it opportunity.

Nuance never lasted long in parking lots. On the bleachers, under a sky that couldn't decide if it wanted to storm, a mother with a perfect ponytail leaned toward Karyn and smiled without warmth.

"Some of us want this more than you do," she said. The sentence landed with the ease of cruelty, like she'd practiced it in the mirror.

Karyn's face went tight. "We want our kid," she said, voice low. "Not a brand."

The mother laughed softly. "Sure," she said. "Keep telling yourself that."

Tyler, standing behind the bleachers, heard it. Jack saw the way the boy's shoulders rose, the way his jaw locked.

"Don't," Jack warned, just a whisper. Tyler stepped down anyway. "You don't know us," he said, voice shaking.

The mother's smile sharpened. "I know the list," she replied. "I know who's serious."

Tyler's eyes flashed. He turned to Jack, and the hurt turned into a weapon. "Maybe you don't know what it takes," he said.

The words were teenage and unforgivable — the kind that make a father see his own failures in a child's face.

Tommy went very still. "I know what it costs," he said. "And I'm not paying with you."

Tyler's nostrils flared. "Then stop deciding for me." Silence opened between them, wide as an outfield. Karyn reached for Tyler, but he stepped back, pride dragging him away.

Tommy watched him walk off into the drizzle and felt something in him crack — not the kind of crack that breaks you, but the kind that changes your shape.

He found Tyler that night out on the back step in his hoodie, the wet of the wood soaking through his jeans, a baseball turning slowly between his hands. The rain had stopped. The streetlight at the corner of Chestnut threw a long pale line down the yard.

Tommy sat down beside him. He didn't say anything for a while.

"I didn't mean it," Tyler said finally, voice rough.

"I know," Tommy said.

That was as much of the apology as either of them needed. They sat with it. After another minute Tommy took the ball out of Tyler's hand and turned it in his own, feeling the seams. Then he handed it back.

"You want to throw?" he said.

They walked into the wet grass — not a lesson, not a speech, just a ball. Tyler threw it back with a careful, honest motion. Tommy caught it. The smack of leather was small and ordinary in the cul-de-sac quiet. They threw maybe ten times. Then Tyler said, "I'm cold," and they went inside.

Chapter Fifteen — The Sandlot Summer

,

IT STARTED WITH A piece of cardboard and a roll of blue painter's tape. Tyler found the box in the garage, cut it flat with a steak knife, and printed the words with a fat black marker until the ink bled:

SANDLOT SUMMER

ALL AGES · ALL ABILITIES VETERANS FIELD

MON / WED / FRI – 5:00 TO DARK

BRING A GLOVE. THAT'S THE FEE.

Kyle added a crooked baseball drawing in the corner. Tyler thought about writing No tryouts. No rankings. but decided the cardboard had said enough.

They hung it on the chain-link fence by the park entrance, the tape wrinkling a little where the metal twisted.

"That's it?" Kyle asked. "That's the big plan?" "That's it," Tyler said. "If people come, they come. If they don't, we still get to play."

Jack, watching from the bleachers with his arms folded, nodded once. "Best marketing campaign I've seen in twenty years," he said. "Short, honest, and priced correctly."

He pointed at the bottom line. Bring a glove. That's the fee. "You'd be amazed how many people don't believe you mean that," he added.

Opening Night

The first Monday looked like every other half-hopeful idea. At 4:45, it was just Tyler, Kyle, Marco, Luis, and Moose Donnelly. Five kids. One big field.

"Worst case, it's really good long toss," Kyle said, dropping his bag in the dugout. Tyler shrugged like it didn't matter, though it did.

By 5:10, two more boys rolled up on bikes, gloves hanging from the handlebars. By 5:20, a minivan door slid open and three younger kids spilled out, their mother calling after them, "If you bleed, wash it at the fountain before you come back!"

No one brought a clipboard. No one brought a bucket of numbered shirts. The only adult on the field side of the gate was Jack, and he leaned against the fence with his hands in his pockets.

"Who's in charge?" one of the younger boys asked. Tyler looked at Kyle. Kyle looked at Marco. Moose shrugged. "Depends what you mean by 'in charge,' " Tyler said. "We're gonna pick teams, make up some ground rules, and if there's a tie, we flip a bat."

The little ones stared.

"What's flipping a bat?" the smallest asked. "You'll see," Marco said. "You'll hate it until you love it." They gathered by home plate, a loose half-circle of hats, hair, and nervous energy. Ages ranged from nine to seventeen. Some wore high school caps. Some wore caps from teams that had long since disbanded. One kid's hat just said Hardware.

"Okay," Tyler said. "We're doing this sandlot style. Two captains. Alternate picks. Nobody gets cut. If you're here, you're on a team."

"And what if it's not fair?" one of the older kids asked, only half joking.

"Then you play harder," Kyle said. "Or make a trade after the first game. We're not building a dynasty. We're trying to play until dark."

They flipped the bat to choose captains. Tyler and Marco won the spin. "First pick," Tyler said, looking over the group. He pointed at a rail-thin twelve-year-old holding his glove like it might break.

"You," he said. "What's your name?" "Evan," the kid said. "You're with me," Tyler said. "You play anywhere you want as long as you hustle." Evan blinked. "Even if I mess up?" he asked.

"Especially if you mess up," Tyler said. The teams formed, lopsided in height and experience, perfectly balanced in eagerness.

"What about umpires?" a parent leaning on the fence called. Tyler shrugged.

"We'll talk it out," he said. "If it gets bad, Jack will squint at us until we remember how to act."

That got a laugh. It also set the tone. No walk-up music. No announcements. No radar guns. Just Tyler lobbing the first pitch of the Sandlot Summer to a nine-year-old whose feet barely reached the back chalk of the box.

The kid swung, missed, and grinned like he'd already won something. They were off.

Learning to Run Their Own Game

The first few nights were rustier than anyone wanted to admit. Halfinning one: a close pitch on the corner.

"Ball," said Kyle from behind the plate. "No way, that's a strike," Moose protested from the batter's box. "Fine," Tyler said from the mound. "We'll call it a strike. Better to hit than walk anyway."

Two innings later: a grounder to short, bang-bang at first. "Safe," said the runner.

"Out," said Moose, now playing first. They argued for forty seconds. Voices rose. Hands flew. Jack let it go just long enough to sting, then cleared his throat. "Remind me," he called. "Who here is getting paid to be right?" Nobody raised a hand.

"So," he said, "you can either stand there and get louder, or you can pick a rule and live with it."

Tyler grabbed the bat. "Flip?" he suggested. Marco nodded. "Ends up, he's safe. Barrel, he's out," Tyler said.

The bat arced through the air, turned once, and clattered to the dirt. Barrel down.

"Out," Tyler said. "Next inning." By the third week, they'd built a whole set of unwritten rules. Two foul balls that hit the big maple = out.

If you show up late, you go to the team with fewer players. If there's a kid under ten in the on-deck circle, everyone moves the fences in a step for him. If you crush one, you go get your own ball.

Older kids took the corners and the deep spots. Younger ones roamed the grass behind them. Somewhere along the way, nobody needed Jack to squint anymore.

They learned how to start a game without a whistle. How to settle a dispute without a grown-up stepping in.

How to keep a score that mattered and didn't at the same time. They changed the teams every couple of nights. Some weeks Tyler and Kyle played opposite each other and tried not to turn it into some unspoken referendum on their futures. Other weeks they played on the same side and spent half their time moving little kids a few steps left or right, calling out, "Back up on this guy!" or "Hey, you cover second if it's hit to me."

The dugouts became confessionals and classrooms.

"Can I pitch?" asked a small lefty one evening, staring at the mound like it was a foreign country. "Sure," Tyler said. "Two batters. If you hit the backstop more than the glove, we'll switch."

The kid hit the glove enough to stay in. After that night, he was a pitcher. Not on a roster. Not in a database. In his own mind.

The only stat that mattered was how quickly he ran back to the mound the next time his team needed an arm.

Parents on the Edges

The parents—some, not all—were the ones who had to learn new habits. They brought their usual chairs out of reflex, then realized there were no lines to check, no bracket to consult, no coach to corner between innings.

Some bounced their knees and checked their phones at first, halfexpecting an app to refresh with an updated score.

Nothing changed. A few kept score in the old way, pencil and paper on their laps, more out of muscle memory than necessity. Most eventually gave up and let the game wash over them.

"Who's winning?" Moose's dad asked one night, genuinely unsure. "Depends what you're counting," Karyn said.

On the bleachers, she kept her own ledger of sorts. Not in a book this time, but in the notes app on her phone.

Wed 6/23 – 19 kids, 3 different ages. Tyler pitched 2, played SS, coached little guy at 2B. Kyle caught 3, laughed more than I've seen in months. No one cried. One scraped knee. No radar guns.

There were still travel tournaments, still showcase emails. Three nights a week, if you drove past Veterans around 7:30, you saw a different kind of youth sports: A kid wearing a faded Bruins shirt trying to lay down a bunt. An eight-year-old in soccer shorts learning to track a fly ball.

Teenagers jogging in from the outfield to high-five a fourth-grader for making a routine catch.

No team banners. No pop-up tents. Just a lot of grass stains and a sound you didn't hear much at complexes: Unscripted laughter.

* * *

BEHIND THE BACKSTOP — A KID NAMED OWEN

The kid had been there for forty minutes before anyone but Kyle noticed him.

He was nine, maybe ten — small for either — and he was sitting on the chain-link rail behind the backstop with his glove in his lap and a tag still on the laces. His bike was leaned against the dugout end, and the bike was too big for him in the way bikes were when somebody had bought it for the kid he'd grow into. He had not asked to play. He had not waved at anybody. He had answered Tyler's "you here for the game?" with a shake of the head so small it was almost a flinch.

Kyle had been catching that night. Three innings in, his knees were tight and his back was talking. He came around behind the backstop to drink water and saw the kid still there, in the same posture, watching the way kids watch when they are figuring out whether they are allowed to want something.

Kyle drank his water. He didn't sit down right away. He leaned on the chain-link a few feet from the kid and looked out at the field with him.

After a minute he said, "You play first base or outfield?"

The kid didn't answer for a long time. Kyle had learned, somewhere along the way, not to fill the silence.

"First," the kid said finally. Then: "Not really. I want to."

"What's stopping you?"

The kid pointed his chin at the field. The current first baseman was Moose, who was six feet of teenager and was at that moment laughing so hard at something Marco had said that he had bent over with his hands on his knees.

"I'd mess up," the kid said.

Kyle nodded slowly. He let the nod do the work for a few seconds. "What's your name?"

"Owen."

"Okay, Owen. Couple of things." He turned and faced the kid, but he didn't crouch down — Kyle had hated, when he was small, the way grown-ups dropped to a knee, like they were going to propose to him. He just stood at the rail. "First thing. Everybody out there has messed up tonight already. Moose dropped a pop-up in the second. That kid in the green hat threw a ball ten feet over my head. I called a strike a ball about an hour ago and I knew it was a strike when I called it. We are all messing up the whole time. That's just what playing is."

Owen looked down at his glove.

"Second thing. I've got a brace on my elbow under this T-shirt. I've had it since I was your age. I caught a season I shouldn't have caught and now my arm makes a click when I put it through a sweater. I tell you that not because it's cool. I tell you that because I figured something out a long time after I should have, which is, you don't get to play if you're scared of what's gonna happen to you out there. Either you go out, or you sit on this rail. Both are choices. The rail is also a choice. I sat on the rail a lot of nights when I was your age."

He paused. He hadn't planned the speech and he was a little startled to hear himself making it. He heard, somewhere underneath his own voice, a different voice — slower, dryer, with a Saugus rasp on the consonants — and he understood, without thinking it through, that he was saying things Jack had said to him on this same chain-link, and that he was saying them in something close to Jack's rhythm. The recognition arrived and passed through him like a chill.

"Third thing," he said, more quietly. "If you go out there tonight and you mess up, I'll be the first guy who tells you it doesn't matter. I'm the catcher. That's literally my job. Fielders mess up, catcher tells them they're fine. You can come over here and we'll work on whatever it was, between innings."

Owen was quiet a long time.

"Tonight?" he said.

"Tonight. Or another night. Or never. Bike's right there. Nobody's going to chase you down."

The kid sat with it. Kyle drank the rest of his water and pretended to watch the game so the kid could decide without an audience.

After a while Owen slid off the rail. He didn't say anything. He walked around the backstop with his glove still in his hand and stood at the edge of the dugout, watching for a hole in the conversation. Marco saw him first and waved him in like he had been expecting him.

When the next half-inning started, Owen was at first base. Tyler had moved Moose to short and was grinning at Kyle from the mound the way Tyler grinned when he caught Kyle being Kyle.

The first ball that came to Owen — a slow grounder up the line — he botched. It went between his legs and rolled to the dugout and a kid scooped it up and tossed it back to him, and Owen looked over at Kyle behind the plate, and Kyle held up two fingers and waggled them, the that one don't count sign Jack had used a thousand times.

The second ball Owen caught.

He stood there with the ball in his glove like he didn't know what to do with it, and Marco yelled, "Throw it home, Owen!" and Owen threw it twenty feet over Kyle's head and into the backstop, and everybody laughed including Owen, and Kyle thought, that was the throw, the one he'll remember, and he felt something in his chest that was not sentiment exactly, more like the click of a thing fitting where it was supposed to fit. He had been waiting his whole life to be on this side of that throw.

He retrieved the ball, lobbed it back to the mound, and crouched again.

He did not tell Tyler about it. He didn't tell Jack. He didn't think it needed telling. He just put it on the page of his head where he kept the things that turned out to matter.

The Game That Sold Out

Word got around. Not online, not at first. Among younger siblings. Among the kids who got cut from travel rosters.

Among the ones who tried the machine and quietly hated it. "Can I come to that Veterans thing?" a boy asked Tyler at school. "Yeah," Tyler said. "Bring a glove. That's the fee."

By mid-July, there were so many kids some nights they had to play two games at once: older ones on the big diamond, younger ones using the right-field grass as a mini-field.

"Who decides which field we're on?" a ten-year-old asked. "The captains," Kyle said. "You'll get your turn. Better learn how you want to run it now."

One Friday, a kid showed up in full travel uniform: white pants, navy piping, expensive cleats, shirt with his last name plastered across the back in tackle twill.

Tyler raised his eyebrows. "Game after practice," the kid explained. "Dad said if I'm going to come here, I have to treat it like 'extra work.' " "Cool," Tyler said. "Work on saying hi, then. You're batting third." The kid tried to bring his travel habits with him at first.

He asked what the exit velo was on a double in the gap. He demanded replays on close calls.

He jogged instead of sprinted. By the fourth inning, he'd forgotten all that.

He slid on a play he didn't need to slide on. He laughed when he popped up and saw the brown streak down his thigh.

He ended the night sitting on the dugout bench in sock feet, travel cleats unlaced, talking to a small boy about how not to be afraid of the ball.

"This place is weird," he told Tyler later. "How so?" Tyler asked. "Nobody's filming," the kid said. "And I'm... having more fun."

"Careful," Tyler said. "You start admitting that out loud, you might not fit in at the next 'can't-miss' weekend."

They both smiled, but the kid's floated somewhere between relief and confusion.

Mary's Ledger, Summer Column

Midway through July, Karyn pulled Mary's old ledger out again. There was a new section now:

Summer 2011 — The Sandlot Summer

Under it, she started a running list.

• Number of travel weekends turned down: 3

• Number of nights we ate dinner together before the field: 9

• Number of new kids who showed up at Veterans because they "heard about the games": 14 and counting

• Number of arm-ice wraps used at home: 0

She added one more line, smiling as she wrote:

• Number of times Tyler came home from the field and said I'm done with baseball: 0

Below the ledger, she kept the Fence Scoreboard open for Tyler and Kyle. Some weeks weren't perfect. Rainouts. Arguments that took too long to settle. Nights when loving the game was a 2 instead of a 3 — somebody's ankle turned, somebody's shoulder barked, a bat met a slump.

But the pattern was unmistakable. Loved the Game: mostly 3s. Impact: mostly 3s. Healthy Enough: stubbornly high.

The Last Night Before School

Summer never ends cleanly. There's no horn. No curtain.

Just one night when the air feels a little different and somebody mentions school supplies.

The last official Sandlot Summer night fell on a Friday in late August. The heat had broken. The light, even at five o'clock, had that sideways, end-of-season slant. Tyler and Kyle got to Veterans early.

They re-chalked the baselines. They dragged the infield. They hung the cardboard sign one more time even though the tape barely stuck anymore. Kids trickled in. The usual crew.

Plus a few new faces determined to squeeze one game in before summer turned into schedules. "Make it a big one," Moose said, slapping his glove. "Last shot before algebra eats my soul." They did.

Captains were chosen by oldest and youngest: Tyler and a nine-year-old named Jayden whose hat kept falling over his eyes. Between the two of them, they built teams that made no sense on paper and all the sense in the world.

They instituted one special rule for the night: "If a younger kid wants to pitch, they get one batter," Tyler said. "No complaining. You had your turn."

Nobody argued. The game that followed was, objectively, a mess. Kids out of position. Balls lost in the lights.

Three errors on one play that still somehow ended in an out. It was also, subjectively, perfect.

When Jayden's one batter dribbled a grounder up the line, Moose charged from first, fielded it barehanded, and whipped it to Kyle covering. Jayden yelled so loud he scared a bird out of the right-field tree.

Later, a skinny kid who'd spent the whole summer saying he "wasn't a hitter" roped a line drive into left. The older boys on both teams cheered, not caring what the scoreboard said.

By the last half-inning, the score was something like 11–10, depending on who you asked and how you counted.

"Bottom of the whatever," Marco called. "Tie game if we want it to be." They let it be.

Two quick outs. Then a walk. Then an infield single.

Then a blooper that fell between three diving fielders— nobody wanted the night to end on a clean play.

Bases loaded. Two outs. Twilight. Jayden came up. Hat crooked. Shirt half-untucked. "Walk-off or bust," Moose shouted from the on-deck circle. "Or both," Kyle added. "We can still play after."

Tyler stood behind the mound, hands on his hips. He toyed with the idea of snapping off something nasty, just to see if the kid could handle it.

Jack's voice floated from the fence. "Make it a pitch he'll remember wanting to hit," he called.

Tyler nodded. He went with something in the generous middle: not a charity toss, not full tilt. Jayden swung with everything in his small frame.

The ball jumped, not far, but far enough—over the pitcher's head, past a diving second baseman, into shallow center where nobody quite got to it in time.

Two runs scored. Three if you counted the kid on first who never stopped running. The dugout emptied.

Jayden was mobbed. Someone yelled, "We just won the Sandlot World Series!" and nobody corrected him.

They played one more inning anyway. Then another half, with a sliver of light left, nobody willing to admit this part of summer was closing.

Finally, the darkness made the decision for them. Tyler stood on the grass near shortstop, hands on his hips, breathing in the last smells of cut field and warm dirt before September turned everything into gyms and weight rooms.

"You good?" Kyle asked, coming to stand beside him. "I'm good," Tyler said. And this time he meant deeply, quietly good, not just I'm fine. They walked off together.

At the fence, the cardboard sign finally surrendered. The tape peeled, and the bottom corner folded over on itself.

Tyler took it down gently and tucked it under his arm. "Keep it," Jack said. "We'll need it again someday." The old man looked out over the now-empty field.

"Place like this doesn't run on banners," he said. "It runs on habits. You built some good ones this summer."

He glanced at the scoreboard, dark and blank. "Funny thing," he added. "Nobody took a picture of that all season, and it's still the truest board we've got."

Kyle laughed softly. "Think we'll miss anything by not being on some National list?" he asked. Tyler thought of the nights under these lights. Of the kids who'd gone from scared to ready. Of the ledger entries and the Fence Scoreboard pages filled with messy, honest numbers.

"Maybe," he said. "But not this." He ran a hand along the top rail where the initials were carved.

The boards waited, as they always did, for whatever initials might come next.

"Next summer?" Jayden called from the parking lot, voice small in the big dark.

"Yeah," Tyler shouted back. "Next summer." The Ruggieros climbed the hill toward home, the cardboard sign under Tyler's arm, dust still on their legs, the sounds of the Sandlot Summer trailing them in echoes. No posts. No rankings. No medals.

Just a field that had remembered how to belong to kids again— and kids who had remembered how to belong to the game.

Chapter Sixteen — College Night at the Field

,

THE IDEA STARTED AT the kitchen table, like most of the good ones had. Karyn had Mary's ledger open to the summer pages. Tommy had the Fence Scoreboard notebook beside it. Tyler and Kyle sat across from them, still smelling faintly of cut grass and sweat from an afternoon at Veterans.

"We keep having the same conversations," Karyn said, tapping the margin where she'd written Sandlot Summer – parents asking how to 'get recruited right'. "At games. At the fence. In grocery lines," Tommy added. "Everybody wants to talk college. Or really, they want to talk scholarships."

Tyler rolled a grape between his fingers. "They ask you, not Coach Rick," he said.

"Sometimes they ask him too," Tommy said. "But they know what he's selling. They think maybe we've seen the other side."

Karyn looked up. "We have," she said. "We've seen the bills. We've seen kids burnt out at sixteen. We've seen a D3 coach show up at a game because he liked a kid's body language more than his 'metrics.' " She flipped to a clean page and wrote a title across the top in neat block letters.

College Night at the Field—To Do

"School auditorium?" Tommy suggested. "Guidance office?" Karyn shook her head.

"No," she said. "Looks too much like a presentation. I want this to feel like what it really is." "What's that?" Kyle asked.

"A reality check for people who love their kids," she said. "We do it at Veterans." Tyler's eyebrows went up.

"At the field?" he asked. "Where else?" she said. "It started with a fence. Feels right that the truth should be told there."

Flyers, Again

A few days later, a new sheet of paper joined the weathered SANDLOT SUMMER cardboard on the entrance fence.

This one was printed at the library, but the words were pure kitchen table:

COLLEGE NIGHT AT VETERANS FIELD

Honest talk for parents and players about baseball after high school. No packages. No fees. No sales pitch.

Guest speakers:

Coach Reilly — North Shore College (Division III)

Coach Miles — Harbor State (Division II)

Coach Jensen — Bay Coast Community (Junior College)

Hosted by Jack Thompson and the Ruggiero family.

Tuesday, 7:00 p.m. Under the lights. Bring a chair.

"Think anybody'll come?" Kyle asked as Tyler taped it up. "Oh, they'll come," Jack said from the bleachers. "Might show up looking for something you're not giving, but they'll come."

"Something like what?" Tyler asked. "A shortcut," Jack said. "We're going to hand them a map instead."

Setting the Stage

The night came in warm and still. Jack dragged the infield out of habit, even though no one would be running bases. The chalk lines glowed like underlined sentences. The big lights over the outfield hummed to life, cutting through the soft early dark.

Tommy and Tyler set up borrowed folding chairs along the first-base line. Karyn arranged a long table behind home plate with a dented coffee urn, cups, and a plate of cookies she'd insisted on baking even when everyone told her it was unnecessary.

"It isn't unnecessary," she'd said. "People listen better if they're holding something."

Kyle taped a hand-lettered sign to the table's front.

NO SIGN-UP SHEETS. JUST QUESTIONS. "Think they'll believe us?" he asked. "They will when they leave with nothing but the truth," Karyn said. By 6:45, cars started to pull into the small lot.

Marco and Luis rolled up on bikes, trailing dust. Moose arrived with his dad, both in work boots. A handful of academy dads came in their quarter-zips, arms folded tight as they scanned the set-up.

Tyler spotted a couple of kids from school travel teams, their mothers walking a step ahead of them with notebooks already in hand.

"Feels like we're about to host a wake," Tommy murmured to Jack. "In a way, you are," Jack said. "A wake for some bad ideas. Might be the healthiest funeral this field has ever seen."

The guest coaches arrived with the easy wariness of men who had learned to be careful where their words ended up.

Reilly came first, in his worn school pullover and a cap that had seen more bus rides than he cared to count.

Miles from Harbor State followed, taller, with the watchful eyes of a man who'd sat in hundreds of gyms and fields, searching for the right kind of flawed.

Jensen from Bay Coast pulled in last, late from practice, still in his fungo shorts and windbreaker, cleats in the bed of his truck.

"Thanks for doing this," Tommy said, shaking each hand. "We're not trying to stir trouble. Just... take some heat out of the room."

"Heat's been turned up for a long time," Jensen said. "About time somebody opened a window."

Jack's Opening

When the chairs were mostly full and the sky had settled into that deep Veterans blue, Jack stepped behind home plate.

He didn't use the microphone Tommy had borrowed from the rec department. He just raised his voice the way he had when he needed left field to hear him in 1979. "Alright," he said. "Welcome."

The field quieted. Even the younger kids, playing catch down the line, turned to listen.

"You all know this place," Jack went on. "Some of you have been coming here longer than you'd like to admit. Some of you are here because your kids dragged you. Either way, I'm glad you made it."

He hooked his thumbs in his pockets and nodded toward the outfield. "This field was built after a terrible night in a restaurant parking lot," he said. "A lot of men swung a lot of hammers so kids could have one patch of dirt where the world made more sense."

He let that sit. "We're not here tonight to sell you anything," he said. "No team. No camp. No 'exposure package.' " A few people shifted in their seats. "We're here because the game's gotten loud and expensive, and a lot of you are losing sleep," he said. "Tonight you get straight answers—from people who don't get a cut of your credit card bill."

He gestured to the table of coaches. "These three gentlemen make their living in college dugouts," he said. "They recruit. They cut. They develop. They watch kids grow up or fall apart. They've agreed to come tell you what they actually look for, what they don't care about, and what really matters between eleven and eighteen."

He pointed to the first row, where Tyler and Kyle sat with a handful of younger kids.

"And these knuckleheads back here are the reason we're doing it on this field," he added. "Whatever you decide after tonight, I want the game to still feel like a gift to them—not an invoice."

A soft laugh rippled through the chairs. Jack stepped aside.

"Coach Reilly," he said. "You're up."

The Numbers, Without the Hype

Reilly walked to the front, calm, but with his chin set.

"I'll keep this simple," he said. "You already get enough complicated." He pulled a crumpled sheet of paper from his pocket but didn't look at it.

"Rough numbers," he said. "Every year, about half a million kids play high school baseball in this country. Of those, maybe 55,000 play some form of college ball. That's all levels. Division I, II, III, NAIA, junior college."

He looked up. "That means roughly nine out of ten good players are done after high school," he said. "Not because they failed. Because that's how the math works."

A murmur moved through the crowd. "At Division I, there are 11.7 scholarships for a roster of 30 or more," he went on. "Some schools fund them all, some don't. Nobody is getting a full ride unless they are a on--in-a-decade arm or some kind of unicorn. Most kids you see on TV are on partial money."

He jabbed his thumb toward his own logo. "At Division III, we don't give athletic money at all," he said. "We give financial aid based on grades and need. I have kids whose packages make it cheaper for them to go to my school than to stay home. Not one of them has 'baseball scholarship' on the envelope. They just have an opportunity."

He let the numbers wash over them for a moment. "So if your only definition of success is 'Division I on TV with a full ride,' you're setting yourself and your kid up for an almost guaranteed heartbreak," he said. "And you're probably going to spend a lot of money chasing that heartbreak."

Miles stepped forward next. "At Division II," he said, "we sit somewhere between his world and the bigger one. We have scholarships, but we stretch them. I might split one scholarship between three guys. Sometimes four. I am not looking for the kid whose family spent the most on tournaments. I am looking for the one who can compete on Tuesdays in March in the cold and still go to study hall."

Jensen, the junior college coach, leaned on the back of an empty chair.

"At my place, we get the kids who were overlooked, or late bloomers, or the ones who needed another year to grow up," he said. "You know what I care about? That they still want to play. That they can pass a class. That they don't think going to a junior college is some kind of failure. Some of my best guys came through a back door and left by the front one."

He folded his arms. "Showcases didn't get them there," he said. "Work and fit did." Questions That Really Mean Fear

Jack stepped back in, clapping his hands once. "Alright," he said. "We could talk at you all night, but that doesn't help much. Let's hear what's actually chewing on you."

A hand went up in the second row. A woman with a notebook already half-filled.

"My son is 15," she said. "Plays on a national team. We spend most weekends on the road. If we pull back, is he going to fall behind? Will coaches stop looking?"

Reilly answered first. "If your son can play, and if he is doing well in school, and if he is reasonably healthy, no," he said. "He will not suddenly vanish from the earth because he is not at every national event."

He smiled a little. "I watched a kid commit to my rival last year," he said. "Great player. I first saw him at a regular high school game on a Thursday afternoon in April. No music. No radar gun on a tripod. His mom was grading papers in the stands. His dad had just come from work. He hit three balls hard and backed up first without being asked. That made my notes. Not the logo on his hat."

Miles nodded. "I recruit the big travel events because it's efficient," he said. "But I'm not fooled. I've watched kids drag their feet between innings, eyes flat, arm hanging like it hurts to lift. I don't care how many national rosters they've made if I see that."

He looked at the woman kindly. "If you pull back from three national teams to one solid team and some good local competition, and your son uses that extra time to get stronger, healthier, and a little happier, you have not hurt him," he said. "You've probably helped."

Another hand, more tentative, went up in the back. Moose's dad.

"My boy is big," he said. "Hits the ball a mile. But his grades are... not great. How much does that really matter if he can play?"

All three coaches answered together. "A lot," they said.

Jensen took it. "If I bring in a kid who cannot stay eligible, I've done him and my program a disservice," he said. "I can help a kid get from a C to a B. I cannot drag a kid who does not care at all. Division II and III coaches, same thing. If we are going to fight for you in a meeting room, we need to know you are fighting for yourself in a classroom."

Reilly nodded. "I have lost count of how many times I've had to cross off a kid I liked because his GPA made our admissions office flinch," he said. "You want to know the cheapest recruiting investment you can make? Get your son or daughter to do their homework."

A third hand, smaller, rose between chairs. It was a boy. Eleven, maybe twelve. Hat too big, ears poking out. "Do I have to play all year to get recruited?" he asked. "Like... winter too? My friend said if I stop, I'll fall behind and never catch up."

The adults shifted, some smiling sadly. Miles crouched a little to see him better. "What's your name?" he asked. "Ryan," the boy said.

"Ryan," Miles said, "here's what you need all year. You need to move your body. You need to eat food that isn't all sugar. You need to sleep. You need to sometimes play baseball. You also need to sometimes play other things. Or play nothing and just be a kid."

He straightened. "If you are seventeen and you love baseball, and you are reasonably healthy, and you are willing to work, I will happily recruit a multi-sport kid who took some winters off from competitive travel," he said. "I will not recruit a kid whose arm is already held together by tape."

Tyler felt that one in his chest. Jack saw it and gave the slightest nod.

Karyn's Ledger

At a pause, Jack waved Karyn forward. "Most of you know Karyn Ruggiero," he said. "She is the one who has actually been keeping track."

The parents laughed. They were used to seeing Tommy pace, Tyler pitch, Kyle catch. They knew less about the woman who rarely missed a game but never raised her voice.

She held Mary's ledger in one hand and the Fence Scoreboard notebook in the other.

"I'm not a coach," she said. "I'm a nurse. I'm also a mom of two boys who have been all through this town's baseball machine. We have done the hotel tournaments and the early flights and the radar gun sessions. We have also sat right out there on Wednesday nights watching pickup games with kids who paid nothing to be here."

She flipped the ledger open. "At some point, we realized we needed something more than our feelings to make decisions," she said. "So we made a list of lines we would not cross. We wrote them in here because that made them feel like a promise."

She read, voice steady. "No playing through real pain. Family gets first claim on weekends some of the time. We will not buy the lie that behind on somebody's list equals behind in life."

She shut the book. "This is not your ledger," she said. "We cannot draw your lines for you. But I wish someone had told us, early on, that we were allowed to have any lines at all. That we were allowed to say no. That saying no to a 'can't-miss' thing did not make us bad parents." She lifted the smaller notebook.

"And this one," she said, "we started when we realized we were losing track of what actually mattered. We call it the Fence Scoreboard.

Three categories: Loved the Game. Healthy Enough. Impact." She smiled faintly.

"There were weekends when the tournament results were great and this board looked terrible," she said. "And there were summers where the opposite was true. Guess which ones I'd like back if I could get them."

She looked out over the crowd, at faces tight with worry, hope, guilt.

"Whatever you choose after tonight," she said, "I hope you make space for a scoreboard like this. It does not show up on a recruiting email. It does show up in who your kid is when the game is over."

She stepped back, the ledger still open in her hand. Tyler and the Kids in the Back

While the adults asked about scholarship percentages and filming every at-bat, Tyler drifted toward the back where the younger kids clustered.

Ryan, the boy who'd asked about playing year-round, stood with Jayden from the Sandlot Summer and a couple of others, all of them halflistening, half-kicking at the dirt.

"You really don't have to play tournaments all winter?" Ryan asked quietly when Tyler got close. "No," Tyler said. "You have to keep getting better. That can look like a lot of things."

"Like what?" Jayden asked. "Like long toss at the field on a Thursday," Tyler said. "Like hitting Wiffle balls in your yard. Like playing basketball so your feet get quicker. Like sleeping. Like not quitting the game because you're tired of airports before you're old enough to drive."

They absorbed that. "But the kids on the big teams..." Ryan started. "...are good," Tyler finished. "Some of them are miserable. Some of them love it. The only question that matters is which group you would be in."

He tipped his head toward the coaches at the front. "You heard them," he said. "They're not scouting your ten-year-old tournament schedule. They're scouting who you are when you're seventeen."

He pointed his thumb at his own chest. "I spent a year thinking I had to do everything," he said. "I pitched too much. I got tired in ways that didn't feel right. And I started to hate the sound of my own walk-up music."

Ryan grinned at that. "You know what fixed it?" Tyler asked. "What?" Jayden said.

"Coming back here," Tyler said. "Playing three nights a week for no reason other than we wanted to. Saying no to one of those big things so we could say yes to a lot of small ones."

He looked out over the field, lights washing the infield in familiar white. "You can chase something without letting it own you," he said. "At least, that's the plan."

The Last Question

Near the end, a father in the front row raised his hand slowly. He wore a work shirt with his name stitched on one side and a small travel team logo on his hat. He looked tired in the way men do when they have been working overtime on things that were never quite explained to them.

"My son is a senior," he said. "We did it all. Tournaments. Showcases. Speed camps. We're sitting on maybe one or two offers from small schools and a lot of 'we'll see.' " He swallowed. "I guess my question is... did we mess up?" he asked. "Should we have done more? Or less? Or different?"

The field went very quiet. Miles answered first.

"Sir," he said, "I don't know you. I don't know your son. I know that if he is a decent kid who can play a little, there is a place for him to keep playing if he wants it badly enough and you can make the numbers work."

He shifted his weight.

"Could you have done things differently?" he asked. "Sure. We all could have. I could have recruited better last year. Reilly could have pulled a pitcher one batter earlier. Jensen could have taken a chance on a kid he passed on. This thing is full of what-ifs."

He looked the man in the eye. "But if you sat in your car at 4:00 a.m. outside a hotel, if you made breakfast, if you talked him through a bad outing instead of tearing him down—you didn't mess up," he said. "You showed up. That counts."

Reilly nodded.

"I've seen kids whose parents did everything 'right' on paper and they still did not get what they thought they wanted," he said. "I've seen kids whose parents did almost everything 'wrong' and the kid ended up exactly where he should be."

He spread his hands. "The only real way to mess this up is to make your kid think your love is attached to a phone call," he said. "If you have not done that, you are ahead."

Tommy felt something unclench in his own chest as he listened. He looked over at Tyler and Kyle, standing by the dugout. At Karyn, ledger in her lap. At the fence that had seen more questions than any recruiting forum ever would.

Jack stepped back to the front one last time. "We're going to shut the lights off soon," he said. "But before we do, I want you to hear one more thing."

He gestured around him. "This field cares about a few simple questions," he said. "Did you show up? Did you play hard? Did you treat people right? Did you leave it a little better than you found it?"

He nodded toward the coaches. "Turns out, that is what most of these college guys care about too," he said. "The rest is details. Some of them very expensive details, if you let them be."

He smiled, small and tired and hopeful. "Go home tonight," he said. "Talk to your kids. Ask them if they like who they are when they are playing this game. If the answer is yes, you're doing more right than wrong." He stepped back.

After Chairs scraped. People lingered in small clusters. Some headed straight for the parking lot, phones already out to text coaches and tweak plans. Others drifted toward the fence, toward the coaches, toward Jack.

Marco's mother thanked Karyn in rapid Spanish and English, alternating between the two when one language did not seem big enough.

Moose's dad shook Jensen's hand for too long.

Ryan and Jayden ran back onto the field to play a quick game of three-flies-up with a couple of older kids who should have been too tired but weren't. Reilly stood near the mound, looking up at the lights.

"Place like this," he said quietly to Tommy, "this is what I hope my guys picture when I say 'remember why you started.' Not some tournament complex."

Tommy nodded. "Thanks for coming," he said. "Send me anyone who loves this view," Reilly said. "I don't care if they never had their name on a national roster."

When the last car pulled out, Jack walked the warning track one more time. The chairs were stacked. The coffee urn was empty. The cardboard SANDLOT SUMMER sign still leaned against the fence, corners soft.

Karyn sat on the bottom bleacher, Mary's ledger open on her lap, phone flashlight balanced between her knees for light.

Under College Night at the Field, she wrote:

• Money collected: $0.

• Programs sold: 0.

• Parents who cried a little: at least 3.

• Kids who stayed to play after: 7.

• Truth told under old lights: enough for tonight.

She hesitated, then added:

• Our boys: still want to come back tomorrow.

She closed the ledger. Tommy flicked the switch in the shed. The big lights buzzed once and went out, leaving only the pale glow from the street.

For a moment, the field was dark. Then a sound floated up from down the right-field line. The soft, unmistakable pop of a ball finding a glove.

Tyler and Kyle, silhouette against the faint sky, tossing one last time before heading home.

No coaches. No clipboards. No talk of offers.

Just two brothers throwing under a dim sky on a field that had generously agreed, for one more night, to be both classroom and sanctuary.

Jack leaned on the fence and listened. "College Night," he said under his breath. "Not a bad use of a Tuesday."

The fence, as always, held its line.

Chapter Seventeen — The Long View

BY THE TIME THE second wave of kids took over Wednesday nights at Veterans, Tyler Ruggiero spent more evenings on buses than under these lights.

Late Summer 2012 · Cedarbrook Field

The grass along the baselines had settled into its familiar late-August tiredness, a little scuffed, a little burned out, still trying. The infield dirt was packed and smooth, the kind of surface that told you a lot of ground balls had already had their say that year.

On the first-base bleachers, Tommy and Karyn sat shoulder to shoulder, coffee cups cooling in their hands. Jack leaned on the fence below them, cap low, hands wrapped around the top rail like it had grown there with him attached.

Out between the lines, the game was in full swing.

Ryan, now taller and all knees, played short. Jayden, whose hat had once swallowed his face, held down second with a pocket full of sunflower seeds. A new batch of nine and ten-year-olds filled out the corners and outfield, shirts untucked, socks mismatched, energy unlimited.

Tyler stood down the third-base line in a faded college T-shirt, hands on his hips, acting as a one-man coaching staff only when asked.

"Two down, runner on first," he called. "If it's hit to you, know where you're going before it gets there."

"We know," Jayden shot back, but he shaded a step toward the hole anyway.

From the fence, Jack watched them with a quiet satisfaction he tried not to show too much. Kids still argued over calls. Somebody still forgot which base to throw to once a night. Nobody checked a phone to see if anyone had posted their exit velo.

"Funny," he said, half to the fence, half to the Ruggieros. "You leave a field alone long enough, kids remember what to do with it."

Tommy smiled. "We didn't exactly leave it alone," he said. Jack grunted.

"Fair point," he said. "But you didn't turn it into a business plan. That counts."

Tyler's Road and the Field's

"Feels weird seeing him down there in that shirt," Karyn murmured. The college logo on Tyler's chest was small, but to her it looked enormous. Not because of the division or the conference, but because the kid wearing it had once needed help getting his foot through the leg of his uniform pants.

"He still looks twelve from back here," Tommy said. "Don't tell him I said that."

They watched as Tyler moved a younger outfielder three steps to his right with one wave of his hand. The kid went reluctantly, then caught the very next ball exactly where Tyler wanted him to be.

"Thank you," Tyler called. "Pay me later." The boy laughed, tossing the ball back in.

"Remember the first time we came here?" Karyn asked. Tommy did. A three-year-old in a sagging cap. A wiffle ball. Jack leaning on the fence like he had nowhere better to be.

"We thought it was just another park," he said. "We had no idea we were signing up for a whole... life."

Karyn sipped her coffee. "We signed up for a few wrong things along the way," she said. "Yeah," Tommy agreed. "But we got some big ones right."

He nodded toward the field. "That kid out there," he said, "still loves this. After all the tournaments. After the showcase emails. After the bus trips. He still comes home and wants to be here."

Karyn watched Tyler tip his hat back the way he did when he was thinking. She thought of the ledger and the Fence Scoreboard, of all the times they'd sat at that same kitchen table and asked, Are we breaking something we meant to bless?

"Long view," she said under her breath. "Guess we're finally far enough out to see some of it."

The New Crew

The game on the field was a hybrid: a little structured, a lot not. They kept score. They ignored it when it got in the way.

"Top seven, we're tied," Ryan announced, even though they weren't. "Everyone hits this inning." "No way, that's not how it works," a twelve-year-old protested.

"Tonight it is," Jayden said. "It's 'Last Friday Before School' rules. You'll understand when you're my age."

"You're thirteen," the younger kid said. "Exactly," Jayden replied. There had been a time when the field needed Jack to start everything. To set the drills. To hit the fungos. To decide when the last ball was in the air.

Now, the older boys ran it. Kyle, catching in a pair of beat-up shin guards he'd once worn in a real tournament, called pitches for a nine-yearold on the mound who still had to think about each step of his motion.

"He doesn't need your nastiest stuff," Kyle told him quietly. "He needs three strikes that don't scare him."

The boy nodded, swallowed, and delivered something approximating that.

Behind the backstop, a few parents lined the fence. Some leaned on the metal, still in work clothes. Some sat on the lowest bleacher with their hands folded, content to be scenery. Nobody wore an academy pullover.

Nobody asked about rankings. The loudest voices were the kids'. "Tag up!"

"Nice swing!" "Hey, you got next batter. Forget that one." The game played on, imperfect and alive.

The Machine in the Distance

Between innings, Tyler jogged to the fence for a sip of water. Jack met him there with a bottle and a question.

"How's college life?" Jack asked. "Busy," Tyler said. "We lift more than we hit some days. Fall ball is... intense." "Good intense?" Tommy asked.

"Mostly," Tyler said. "Different kind of noise. Less walk-up music, more coaches with clipboards."

He shrugged. "It's a lot of work," he said. "But when I close my eyes and think about what I love about it... it still looks like this place."

He nodded toward the field. "Pretty much why I keep coming back," he added. Out beyond the tree line, if you looked hard enough, you could see the faint glow of the academy's lights. The building was busier than ever. Their social media posts, when they floated across local feeds, carried slogans about "Next-Level Exposure" and "National Track Pathways."

Kids still went there. Some of tonight's players had a foot in both worlds.

"Got fall tournaments lined up?" Jack asked. Tyler nodded.

"Coach has us at a couple of big ones," he said. "Says it's less for recruiting and more to see how we handle playing three games in a day against good arms."

He rolled his shoulder. "It's fine," he said. "I just have to remember it's part of the job, not the whole point."

Jack's eyes crinkled. He didn't say anything. He just nodded once, the small nod he used when a kid had said something he might have said himself.

Tyler tapped the fence rail. "I like this soundtrack better," he said. From the field, Jayden hollered, "Ty, we need a runner! Old man Reyes pulled a hammy." "You're nineteen, you punk," Marco shouted back.

Tyler grinned and jogged out, water bottle in hand. Jack watched him go for a moment, then turned back toward the bleachers.

Ledger Math

On the bleachers, Karyn had Mary's ledger balanced on her knees, pen tucked behind her ear. "You brought it?" Tommy asked, glancing over.

"I needed to settle something with myself," Karyn said. She flipped back through pages that smelled faintly of old paper and coffee. Tournament weekends. Sandlot Summers. College Night entries. Fence Scoreboard tallies.

"So?" Tommy asked. "So when I started this, I thought I was keeping track of baseball," she said. "Turns out I was keeping track of us."

She turned to a fresh page and began a new section. 2012 — The Long View. Under it, she wrote slowly: Tyler: playing college ball, still coming home to Veterans when he can. Kyle: healthy, catching again on his terms, mentoring the little ones without realizing that's what it is. Machine: still loud. Field: still here.

She closed the ledger and put it beside her on the bench. "I'm not sure Mary ever intended it to be this," she said. "But I think she'd approve."

Tommy followed her gaze to where Tyler was laughing at first with Jayden after a bad throw and an unnecessary dive.

"Mary liked honest work," he said. "This qualifies."

Jack's Hand-Off

The game wound down the way sandlot nights always did.

Not with a horn or an umpire's last call, but with the light getting harder to read and a parent on the hill glancing at a watch.

"Last half-inning!" Kyle called. "For real this time." They played it out.

A bloop. A grounder. A swing that missed by a foot and still earned a pat on the back.

When it finally ended in what half the kids insisted was a tie and the other half insisted was a win for their side, nobody seemed inclined to argue too hard.

Bats were leaned against the dugout wall. Gloves got stuffed into bags. Dirt shook off cleats. Tyler and Kyle lingered near home, looking out at the field the way their father and Jack did. "Hey," Jack called from the fence. "You two."

They walked over. Jack held up a small ring of keys. Fence gate. Shed. Lights. "I'm not going anywhere," he said. "But I'm not going to live forever either, despite what some of these little maniacs seem to think."

He pressed the keys into Kyle's palm. "Consider this an advance on your adult responsibilities," he said. "Somebody's going to need to open up and drag this place when the next crop of kids shows up. Might as well start training you now."

Kyle stared at the keys, their weight suddenly visible in his hand. "Are you sure?" he asked.

"No," Jack said. "But I'm doing it anyway." He nodded at Tyler.

"You're going to be off chasing balls in bigger parks," he said. "Good. Somebody from this town should. But don't forget where to send the kids who look like they're getting chewed up. And don't forget you've got a brother who might need someone to haul the chalk bags once in a while."

Tyler swallowed. "I won't," he said.

Jack clapped each of them on the shoulder. He didn't say anything else. He nodded once toward the right-field corner, where the carved initials caught the last of the light.

"You boys figure out when and where you want your names on there," he said. "Don't rush it. Let the field tell you when you've earned it."

He turned back toward his truck, then paused. "And for the love of God," he added over his shoulder, "don't let anybody hang a banner out here with a website on it. I will haunt you."

Kyle laughed. "Deal," he said.

A New Carving

A week later, on a cooler evening that smelled like school and new notebooks, Tyler and Kyle came down to Veterans with a flashlight and a pocketknife.

"No one asked us to," Kyle said. "I know," Tyler replied. "That's kind of the point, right?" Kyle added.

They walked to the right-field corner where the boards had weathered but held. The old initials felt deeper now.

Kyle ran his fingers under them, feeling the grooves. "Feels wrong to add ours," he said. "Like we're cutting in line." Tyler shook his head.

"Fence is big enough," he said. "And this isn't about us being special. It's about saying we're part of whatever this has been all along."

He flipped open the knife and, with more care than he'd show anything else all week, carved two new sets below the old ones.

They weren't as neat. The wood flaked a little at the edges. The letters leaned. "Mary would fix those," Kyle said.

"Yeah," Tyler said. "She would." They stepped back. In the flashlight beam, the four sets of initials looked almost like a timeline you could touch.

"Think anyone will ever care?" Kyle asked. "About these?" Tyler said. "Maybe not. About what they stand for? I hope so."

He clicked the light off. For a moment, the corner disappeared into the dark.

Behind them, from the infield, came the sound they knew better than any scholarship offer or radar reading.

Kids laughing. Ball hitting glove. Someone yelling, "I've got it!" a beat before they really did.

Tommy and Karyn sat on the first-base bleachers, leaning into each other, watching this new group try to figure out which way to run and when to let a little kid have an extra swing.

Jack, perched on the top row with his hands folded on his cane, watched the whole scene with the same steady eyes he'd turned on this field for decades. From up there he could see the creek, the hill, the faint glow of the academy across the marsh, the worn baselines, the kids sprinting nowhere in particular and everywhere at once.

Down below, Ryan yelled, "Last one, make it count!" The ball rose into the evening, hung for a moment against a sky that had seen all of this before, then dropped toward a waiting glove.

Caught. Nobody cheered particularly loud. They didn't need to.

The inning ended. The kids stayed. The adults watched.

Epilogue — The Kids in the Dark

EVEN WITH THE LIGHTS off, Cedarbrook never stayed dark for long when kids were on it.

Late September, years after the first sign-up night in the cafeteria. Years after the big tournament weekends and the ledger lines that ran into the margins. The air had that edge it got when summer finally surrendered. Breath showed for the first time in weeks. Jackets came out of trunks. The mosquitoes, mercifully, gave up.

The game should have been over an inning ago. "Last one," Kyle had called from behind the plate, voice hoarse. "Make it count."

He had said it three innings in a row. Now he stood at the backstop without his gear, mask hanging on a post, a half-circle of nine, ten. And eleven-year-olds spread across the field like spilled marbles. Tyler leaned on the fence near first, shoulders loose, college logo on his chest faded from too many washes.

The lights hummed overhead, then flickered once in warning. Ten minutes, the field seemed to say. Last call.

Ryan, older now, manning shortstop with the comfortable gait of someone who had finally grown into his own arms and legs, yelled, "Two outs, bases loaded, tie game."

Nobody had checked the score in three innings. That was the kind of game it had turned into.

A kid named Malik stepped into the batter's box, batting helmet slightly crooked. He was new to the town, new to the field, new to the feeling of thirty pairs of eyes on his back that were not asking for grades or chores, just for a swing.

"Relax," Tyler called. "It's just a ball and a stick. You've been doing some version of this since you were two."

Malik grinned, tugged at his gloves like he'd seen big leaguers do, and dug in.

Kyle lobbed one in from the mound, the kind of pitch that sat exactly in the space between challenge and kindness.

Malik swung. The ball leapt off his bat on a line toward the right-center gap.

Two kids took off after it, shouting over each other. The ball split them by inches, rolled to the fence, and rattled against the boards where four sets of initials sat carved in an uneven column.

"Run!" everyone screamed, though Malik was already flying, arms pumping, legs churning. He touched first, second, third, hat flying off somewhere in the chaos, and dove across home in a tangle of limbs and laughter.

Safe. Out. It didn't matter. They piled on him anyway.

"All-time walk off," Jayden announced, even though he declared at least three walk offs a month.

The lights flickered again. This time, they went out. The sudden dark drew a chorus of oohs and one dramatic scream from a kid who liked the sound of his own voice.

For a second, nobody moved. The field, without its lamps, felt bigger and stranger. The sky pressed down a little closer. The town glowed faintly beyond the trees.

Then phones came out, small squares of light blinking on, cutting loose circles in the dark.

"Do not," Kyle said, "and I mean this, do not throw a ball right now." "Yeah," Tyler added. "We like all of you with the same number of teeth you came in with." There was laughter, shuffling, the familiar slap of gloves being found and stuffed into bags. "Alright," Kyle continued. "That's it. For real. Pack it up. School tomorrow."

Groans all around. "Can we come Friday?" Ryan asked. "And Sunday?" Malik added. "And next Wednesday?" a smaller kid asked. "Even if it's cold?"

"Yes," Kyle said, before anyone else could answer. "If there's no snow on the ground and somebody can find the key, this place is open."

He patted his pocket where the ring of shed and light box keys had lived for a few years now.

"Somebody will find the key," Tyler said quietly. Jack sat halfway up the bleachers, cane balanced across his knees, jacket zipped. The years had bent him around the edges. But his eyes had not dulled. He watched the cluster of kids moving through the half-light, watched the way they bumped shoulders and shared gear and shoved each other toward the parking lot.

"What are you thinking?" Karyn asked, stepping up to sit beside him. Tommy came to stand at the rail below, coffee in hand.

Jack rested his palm on the bleacher beside him, feeling the cool metal through his glove. He didn't answer for a while.

"I'm thinking they don't need me out here as much as they used to," he said. "Which is mostly the point."

Karyn smiled.

He looked toward Tyler and Kyle, who were finishing a slow walk around the bases with a couple of younger kids trotting at their sides, hanging on every word of some half-true college story.

The kids, packed into the parking lot now, made their own light. Car headlights opened and closed. Doors thudded. Voices overlapped.

"Practice on Saturday?" "Bring your cousin next time." "Coach Kyle, can you show me that backhand thing again?" "Ty, is it true you hit one over the scoreboard at college?"

"Once," Tyler said. "Wind was blowing out. Don't tell the story any bigger than it was."

They drifted off in ones and twos, taillights disappearing up Chestnut Street.

When the last engine noise faded, Cedarbrook Field went quiet in the way only a place with good secrets can.

Tommy and Karyn gathered the stray water bottles and a hoodie someone would have to come back for. Jack stood carefully, leaning on his cane, and made the slow walk along the warning track toward the rightfield corner.

He rested one hand on the carved initials. "Still here," he said softly.

Tommy and Karyn caught up. They stood with him a moment in the dark.

"Think it will last?" Tommy asked.

Jack didn't answer right away. He patted the board. "This," he said, "will last as long as somebody is willing to unlock the gate and throw a ball until it's too dark to see it."

Karyn slipped her arm through Tommy's. "Mary used to say there would always be kids in the dark," she said. "Not because the lights broke. Because this world keeps inventing new ways to make them feel like they're behind."

Jack nodded. "Then we better keep the boards tight," he said.

They walked back toward the lot together. Behind them the field settled in. The baselines blurred. The mound cooled.

Somewhere beyond the outfield, a car door shut. A final engine turned over. The sound drifted away.

Then, from the street, a young voice floated back through the trees. "See you Wednesday!"

The field did not answer. It just waited.

Author's Note

The events of this book are imagined. The town is not.

I grew up on a field like Cedarbrook. Not the same field — that one had a different fence, a different creek, a different set of names carved in a different right-field corner — but the same kind of place. The kind a few people built because somebody had to, and then a few more people kept showing up to keep it standing. I have been a kid on a field like that, and I have been a parent watching kids on a field like that, and somewhere in the middle of those two I started writing about what we owe the places that ask nothing of us except that we close the gate behind us when we go.

The youth-baseball world this book describes is not invented either. The academies, the showcases, the radar-gun readings, the can't-miss emails arriving at six in the morning, and the parents trying to do right by children who cannot yet tell them what they need — that culture is real, and it is larger every year. I have nothing against the people inside it. Many of them are coaches I respect, working hard inside a system that pulls in directions they did not choose. The book is not an argument with them. It is a record of one family trying to figure out which parts of that culture to take and which parts to set down, and a record of one small field that kept offering an alternative for as long as anyone was willing to drag the infield.

The Ruggieros are made up. So are Jack and Carver and Coach Reilly and Marco and the rest. The fence and the carved initials are made up too, although I have spent enough time with my hand on old boards to know the difference between a fence that keeps people out and a fence that asks people to come back.

This is the third book in The Sandlot Series, following the prequel, Beneath the Home Run Sky, and Books One and Two, The Sandlot

Promise and The Sandlot Legacy. Thank you for reading, and for caring about the kind of game these books are trying to remember.

— Walter A. Beede

Saugus, Massachusetts

A Note on the Series

The Sandlot Spirit is Book Three of The Sandlot Series.

Beneath the Home Run Sky is the prequel. It reaches back to the River Works years, the first rough shape of Cedarbrook Field, George's early field log, and the family history that gives the fence its deeper meaning.

The Sandlot Promise is Book One. It begins in the winter of 1969–70, after the night of December 27, 1969, when the lives of two Saugus families changed in a parking lot off Route 1. Officer Arthur Belmonte was killed in the line of duty that night. Officer Frederick Forni was wounded and survived. Their families have given me their permission to refer to them by name. I am grateful beyond measure. The book is dedicated to them.

The Sandlot Legacy is Book Two. It follows George Davis, Cedarbrook Field, and Jack Thompson through the years when the field's future is challenged and its meaning is tested.

The Sandlot Spirit is Book Three. It picks up the same field a generation later, as the Ruggiero family navigates what youth baseball has become.

These books can be read in chronological order beginning with the prequel, or in publication order beginning with The Sandlot Promise. Each one stands on its own, but together they tell the story of a field, a fence, and a promise passed from one generation to the next.

— W. A. B.

Acknowledgments

To the Belmonte and Forni families: thank you for trusting me with names that belong to you. I have tried to be careful with them. I will keep trying.

To Bret Saberhagen, who agreed to write the foreword to The Sandlot Promise: thank you for taking the time, and for understanding what these books are trying to say.

To the early readers — you know who you are — thank you for telling me what worked and what didn't, and for being patient with how many drafts it took for me to listen.

To Saugus: thank you for the field.

www.ingramcontent.com/pod-product-compliance
Lightning Source LLC
LaVergne TN
LVHW040220110826
845146LV00005B/1352

* 9 7 9 8 9 9 5 7 1 1 3 0 8 *